TOO BIG

by

Gary Tarulli

to my wife
forever young

Too BIG: Gary Tarulli

CONTENTS

PREFACE

I SHALL TELL YOU the story of John Whitmore, a man who became too big and, in the process, was compelled to become too famous. Social media is pervasive, and it does not tolerate anonymity well.

And yet, despite—and because of—his notoriety, a complete picture of John is sorely lacking. I shall remedy that fault, for the close association he and I share has allowed me to go where the public has little or no access. I will describe what happened in real life, going beyond the man's remarkable physical transformation to reveal his distinguishing character.

Others would have preferred to be left unexposed. To them, I say sorry, not sorry. They are the bad actors and trolls in the media and elsewhere who make fact and fiction indistinguishable through their deceptions, distortions, and lies. Conjure a conspiracy theory, and legions of people will blindly follow, like lemmings hurling themselves off a cliff. Post a lie, it goes viral and becomes gospel—the new religion of the duped.

The struggle is real. We respond to the nonsense by becoming cynics, wrapping ourselves in a cloak of skepticism that too often keeps out what is true. The alternative, to be naive and uncritical, is to wander through life naked and suffer the consequences.

The few remaining doubters of John's story may seek a mystical explanation for what transpired. Was it not Shakespeare who penned that there are more things in Heaven and Earth than are dreamt of in your philosophy? Others, devotees of science, might look for the reason in a multiverse of infinite realities.

One thing is sure: John's increase in size is not the most important aspect of what you will read. What is more instructive is the type of troubles he faced and how he responded.

1. IN THE BEGINNING

TO BEGIN. BEFORE HIS life turned upside down, John might have been considered an ordinary person leading an everyday life. I do him no disservice in this seemingly banal characterization, for unless you stood on the moon and giddily grinned back at Earth or relinquished your cell phone for an entire hellish month, living such a life might describe the best of us. Ordinary, however, does not necessarily mean basic. At any given moment, as you shall soon see, we are all capable of doing some crazy shit.

John is forty-one years of age—a millennial. But like an increasing number of that generation, he has accumulated a wife, a couple of kids, and a house that is goals. You'll only find a Subaru Ascent in his two-car, not a sportier whip, but sacrifices must be made when there's a fam to haul about. Until recently, he had a well-paying job, meaning he would never have to skip a mortgage payment to fund his daughter's future Sweet Sixteen party or raid his 401(K) to fund his kids' college education. On weekends, he certainly didn't *have* to mow his half-acre lawn (landscaping crews were swarming like locusts all over his suburban neighborhood), but he did so anyway—but only for the exercise.

He and I met during the first few days of college before classes began in earnest. Like most out-of-control first-year students, we behaved like idiots. To set a fitting example, we coerced the two wings of our L-shaped dorm to declare war on each other. As enemy combatants, we were entrenched at opposite ends of a long hallway, manning cannons fashioned from empty, overturned beer kegs. That he and I could happily partake in such stupidity was fodder for a lasting friendship.

As we grew older, our common philosophy was not to take life too seriously. It doesn't overtax the imagination to understand why someone like me could stumble into an unpredictable career as a freelance journalist. John's choice of a business-oriented path had more to do with family. Such things have a way of mellowing a person, but there are still times when my friend strays down the path of lunacy, and I'm right there with him.

One of my friend's best attributes is a heightened, unassuming sense of humor. I'm convinced that was how he faced what happened to him with such astounding composure. An example comes to mind. It occurred during winter break at a ski resort in New York's Adirondack Mountains. Being labeled a novice skier never stops someone young from taking foolish risks. On a black diamond mogul, my friend took one too many, lost control, cartwheeled, took an eternity of air time, and disappeared into the snow-laden forest. I found him on his back, covered in powder, with skis stuck in a drift, pointing at a clear blue sky. "A teachable moment," he managed to gasp through a fog of frozen vapor. When I stopped laughing, I removed my gloves and immortalized the moment with my cell.

I sent him the photo. Later, I found it on Myspace. He had added: "My Best Day Skiing."

Another example involved a car accident. The other driver was a young woman whose too-big SUV was virtually unscathed. Not so, my friend's crumpled, overturned MINI C.

Frightened, the woman knelt to peer into his car, saying:

"My God, are you all right?!"

"Either the world's upside-down, or I am."

"I'm so, so sorry! Are you sure? What shall I do?!"

"One small thing," he said, crawling out of the car's shattered window and shaking glass from his hair and coat. "Could you give me a lift?"

The young woman involved, Amanda, told me the words.

She became John's wife.

Stories such as these are key to understanding how he handled his rapid change in appearance.

Like you and me, he started tiny, about 100 microns, the size of a fertilized human egg cell. He made his entry into this world as a healthy eight-pound baby boy. By age six, he was forty-seven pounds with no hint of the unusual changes to come. At ten, when he weighed sixty pounds, his unknowingly prescient mom scolded: "John, you're getting too big for your britches!"

Thirty-one years later, there wasn't a pair of britches on the planet that would fit him.

When we first met, John was a hair shy of six feet tall and weighed 177 pounds. He remained near this ideal weight until the onset of his affliction—a noteworthy achievement for a married American male in his forties.

Before his atypical increase in height and weight, people would notice his piercing brown eyes, thick, straight brown hair that showed no evidence of receding, and lightly tanned skin that refused to fade with the advent of winter thanks to time spent outdoors. Unless you live on a mountaintop in Tibet, you'll know this from his constant presence in the media. Handsome and physically fit says it all, and I once benefited. In fondness and remorse, I recall the days when I was John's wingman—days now glimpsed in the rearview mirror.

With wild oats properly sown, John went on to greener pastures while my pasture, until recently, lay fallow.

A word about me. Despite my friendship with John, I remain less known to the public. In size and popularity, he literally and figuratively overshadowed me. I can't imagine anyone giving a damn about my appearance. Because it is difficult to disprove a negative, I'd say I'm not bad to look at.

Although you can't judge a book by its cover, you often can get a good idea by getting to know its author. Simply put, the world I see spinning out of control has colored my outlook, and all that prevents me from becoming a pessimist is that I consider my participation in this sanitarium called Earth to be some cosmic joke. I await the punch line. I have been variously described as a free spirit, a loner, and anti-social, though never quite rising to the ranks of sociopath. I have been capable of liking any one *person* (some of my best friends are human), but not nearly as capable of liking *people*.

John is different, and his tolerant approach to society's more annoying conventions positively affects the people around him. You will see I have not been entirely immune to this generosity of spirit.

Why is any of this important? A good editor once told me that characters in a story need "to have skin in the game." John, due to his largeness, has plenty. But while he transitioned in size, in fundamental ways, he remained very much the same. I, on the other hand, went from almost being labeled a sociopath to something a bit different.

In the end, you will also come to appreciate that what transpired was so far out of the ordinary that it engendered a correspondingly unconventional reaction in both of us.

2. DOCTOR VISITS

MY STRANGE ODYSSEY WITH John started nearly at the beginning of his difficulty. By chance, I was present during the doctor's office visit when he had the first inkling of the remarkable transformation he would undergo. I was there because the appointment he had scheduled months prior conflicted with another recently made: the 30,000-mile warranty service on his car. Since his wife worked regular hours, and I do not, I offered him a lift.

John and Amanda's home is located in a "good" neighborhood. Another word is "upscale." In suburbia, this typically means larger lots, sidewalks no one ever uses, and well-lighted streets that somehow make residents feel safe. To enjoy these perks, you can expect to find stratospheric home prices and higher, soul-sapping property taxes.

John was fortunate to have purchased his home before prices went through the roof. Existing homeowners had the illusion of wealth, which was dispelled when a variable-rate home equity loan, insurance, and taxes came due. The monthly payments for new home buyers became too big, effectively shutting out some Millennials and most Gen Zers from that aspect of the American Dream. Even John could not have afforded his home without the aid of his wife, who was gainfully employed. She didn't mind working. If only it could have been in the same field as her two-hundred-thousand-dollar, four-year-plus-one master's degree, which burdened the family with a loan she derisively referred to as a second mortgage.

Like most homes in modestly affluent neighborhoods, the Whitmores' front door was monitored by a motion-activated, infrared, heat-seeking, hi-def, wide-angle camera, which told me I didn't need to knock. The damn thing probably knew I had arrived before I did.

A beautiful face full of freckles and a squall of copper-colored hair came to the front door. I have known Amanda for twenty years. There is a wine variety called Tempranillo that is said to age well. That would be her. You drink her in.

"Thanks a shit-ton for doing this," she said, greeting me with a warm hug. "I've been taking trash from my dick of a boss for missing way too much work ... you know, because of the kids."

I had my usual platitude ready. "Hey, no problem, that's what friends are for." Anticipating me, we said the last words together and then laughed together.

John suddenly appeared. He feigned anger. "You flirting with my wife again?"

I was a bit jealous of John, but it was of the healthy type. "You'd both be insulted if I didn't," I answered. "By the way, where are the kids?"

"Walking to school," Amanda replied.

"Really?!" I said, feigning alarm. "Kids walking to school?" When I drove up, every third corner had children at the bus stops, guarded by a parent in an SUV.

"They walk together," John informed me. There were two preteens, a boy and a girl. Gen Alpha's. It is said that a child born after 2025 will, from birth, be so thoroughly absorbed by technology and social media that they will require no special designation. In my admittedly limited experience with children, what defines all kids is their ability to be socially anxious and assertive at the same time.

John and I said goodbye to Amanda and began our

excruciatingly slow drive to the doctor's office. Traffic was heavy, with nine-to-fivers going to work and the work-at-homers traveling whenever they pleased. Judging by the vacant look on many faces, few seemed eager to go anywhere.

To pass the time, I waved to a woman in a too-big SUV trapped by traffic in the next lane. She was on her cell while simultaneously doing her nails. I powered down my window and shouted, "Where's a good manicurist when you need one?" I knew she wouldn't smile. On the plus side, she didn't flip me off.

"I once saw a man shave his bald head," John commented.

"Shaving cream or electric?"

"Fair question. Electric."

The practice of Dr. Sanjay was in a large 'medical park' with offices that administered to every body part known to man, woman, or gender of your choosing—a half-square-mile healthcare version of the Shopping Mall of America.

Our destination was a one-story building made to look important with two-dimensional white columns. After a short introductory conversation with a young, disgruntled receptionist (they always seem to be), we situated ourselves in the waiting room. The air conditioning system overcompensated for the atypically hot day, wasting energy. Most offices are like this.

I looked at John and commented, "I think I can see my breath."

"Same. I've lost all feeling in my extremities."

"I'm afraid to close my eyes," I said. "They might freeze shut."

We waited. There was little decoration to command one's attention. Hanging loosely on one wall was a faded photo of a sailboat silhouetted by an orange sunset. Spewed on a nearby table were boating magazines. The mags eliminated during COVID were slowly making their way back. Not a pity: No trade mags detailing how to turn a tree trunk into a coffee table.

We waited some more. I needed a way to amuse myself. Four

other souls were similarly interred. Across from me was an elderly gentleman who hadn't moved in quite some time. He appeared to be silently dozing. Or he had frozen to death. One seat from him sat a mother tapping on her cell, ignoring her squirming child, a five-year-old boy. When she wasn't looking, I made a silly face at the brat. He responded in kind. Silly faces went back and forth until the mom sternly told her son to stop bothering me. He protested the unequal justice and was reprimanded. Who said "life was fair," I felt like telling the boy. When mom wasn't looking, but the kid was, I made a silly face at her.

After an hour, John looked up from his cell and said, "Do you think anyone would mind if I brought in my sleeping bag next time?"

I smiled. "That would be too subtle."

We were ready to bounce when John was called in and told me to follow. After another fifteen minutes of waiting, an assistant entered and did what many general practitioners once did: took blood pressure, temperature, and pulse ox, then asked (don't bother to measure) weight and height. If you're over seventy, they ask if you've fallen recently.

Dr. Sanjay rapped on the door, entered, sat, and opened his laptop. I wondered if he was checking his stock portfolio or surfing the Net for a stainless doodad (remembering the waiting room photo and mags) for the sailboat he owns. A quick physical exam revealed him to be a man in his mid-fifties with silver, thinning hair and a face that was etched enough to look experienced. He was entering the autumn of his life, I'd say mid-October in the Northern Hemisphere. I fixated on his most prominent feature, bushy caterpillar eyebrows that I half-expected to morph into moths and flitter away.

There was no reason to suspect anything out of the ordinary would transpire, which was wrong, for it would be the first time John gave voice to what would soon take over his life and make him the object of public scrutiny. Fortunately for me, he has a good memory and a habit of using his cell phone to record doctor visits. Not long

10

afterward, I did my own recording.

"Morning, Doctor," John began. "Or is it afternoon by now?"

Sanjay interrupted his phubbing. "Couldn't be helped. Another emergency." It's the usual vague way of a doctor apologizing, but you seldom get even that level of repentance, no matter how long you're kept waiting. The real reason is the overbooking of patients.

"I see you have your cell phone out," Dr. Sanjay said, looking at John. "Recording our visit?"

"You've never objected before," John responded.

The doctor surprised me: "And I don't now—no reason to. There would be fewer malpractice cases if people recorded what their physicians actually said instead of what they thought they said or wanted to hear. Anyway, what brings you in today? The aide mentioned that you were worried about gaining a couple of pounds. Tut-tut. Welcome to middle age."

"Yeah, I get it. But it is a bit unusual for me. Shirt's getting a little tight."

"I see you have a marginal weight increase, one seventy-seven to one eighty-one. Four pounds since your last visit. Nothing out of the ordinary. Otherwise? Feeling ok? Your blood pressure is normal. Your BMI is 19.2, excellent for a man your age. Life insurance companies should be paying you."

Rising, Dr. Sanjay placed the stethoscope on John's back, then listened as his patient drew in deep breaths. After feeling for a pulse at the ankles, he asked John a few questions to rule out signs of depression. The doc appeared disinterested, and I couldn't blame him much: This patient wasn't presenting much of a challenge to all those years of medical school and internship.

"You're healthy," came the diagnosis.

"I feel pretty good," John had to admit.

Sanjay was temporarily called out of the room. "You like this doctor?" I asked John. "Why?"

"I do. You'll see."

Sanjay stepped back in. "No advice concerning the weight?" John asked, with a nod to me. "Can you recommend a diet?"

"Have you altered your eating habits? Are you consuming more alcohol?"

"No, should I?"

"A waist is a terrible thing to mind," I inserted.

"Clever," John said.

Sanjay merely raised a bushy caterpillar. It's hard to get physicians to laugh, or so I have often found.

"Perhaps a ketogenic diet?" Sanjay recommended. "Increase your fats and cut out your carbohydrates. There are quite a few adherents."

"Not for me. I'm part Italian. Giving up pasta would be like withdrawal."

"There's nothing like a good plate of pasta fazool," I volunteered, only because I liked the way the sound came rolling off my tongue.

"There's the Paleo diet."

"Eat as a caveman might?" John asked. "My wife tried it. Started brandishing a wooden club."

I chuckled. The doctor's eyebrow fluttered. He persisted: "There's intermittent fasting. In prehistoric times, humans went without eating for several hours, sometimes days."

"I get to carry my own club?" John asked.

I laughed. Dr. Sanjay had more diets at his disposal. "If it fits your macros," he offered. "I-I-F-Y-M. A regimen of consuming a specific percentage of each macro food group. Carbs, some fats, and fewer proteins."

"The opposite of the Keto diet?" John protested. "Too complicated. I'd need a math degree and a calculator."

"Vegan?" Sanjay suggested.

"I don't think I could follow that one, Doc, but my friend Max sees merit in fewer cows farting methane."

"I imagine," Sanjay replied, "he wouldn't appreciate the carnivore diet."

"That's really a thing, Doc?" I asked.

"Yes, 'it's a thing.' Lots of meat, cheese, fruits, and veggies."

"Brought to you," I said, frowning, "by the dedicated culinary research team at McDonald's."

Sanjay then went on an impressive rant, citing Mediterranean, OMAD, DASH, and several other diets. When John ruled them all out, the doctor made one final attempt. "There's the dessert with breakfast diet," he said. "Eggs and a slice of cake."

"Ok, we probably deserved that," John said with a grin, believing, as did I, that Dr. Sanjay was exhibiting a sense of humor.

"It's a thing, John," Sanjay insisted. "It's just what you seem to need. You can have your cake and eat it, too."

As John expected, I was schooled. Sanjay proved smarter than I gave him credit for, *and* he had a sense of humor. Having better things to do than entertain us, he made signs to leave. Good. Between the long wait and food talk, I was feeling hangry.

John rose to his feet. Hesitating, almost as an afterthought, he said, "One more quick thing, doc. Do people continue to grow when they are forty-one? Could I be getting a little taller?"

"Well... the short answer is 'no,'" Sanjay replied. "Males stop growing by age twenty or sooner. Upon waking, you may be a centimeter or so taller before the effects of gravity and weight compress the discs in your spine. I see you are not happy with my answer. Get on the scale."

With one eye on me and an expression of 'sorry to put you through this,' my friend complied.

"Six feet one and a half inches," the doctor said, reading the scale's digital display.

For the briefest moment, a cloud of concern darkened my friend's face. "I thought you said we're *shorter* later in the day?" he asked.

"So I did."

"I've never been over six feet."

"You don't say?" Sanjay said, not quite believing. "A likely explanation is that all scales can give slightly different readings between calibrations. Or perhaps the aide reading the scale rounded down the last number from your visit six months ago."

Sanjay's answer didn't quite satisfy my friend. What appeared to worry him was that the doctor had an odd look on his face. Was the expression one of curiosity mixed with incredulity?

As we left, the woman at the front counter handed John a referral for a specialist. Smiling as he signed the credit card slip for the co-pay, he said, "I'm billing you for two hours of my time."

A half-smile came back, along with, "You can try."

Sanjay called in a favor, and we were on our way to a specialist.

"Say again?" I asked. Startled, I sought clarification.

"Your car seat's memory," John replied. "I had to alter my sitting position, moving the seat back and down."

I couldn't ignore what that implied. For the first time, I observed a noticeable increase in John's size—something faintly approaching the look of Barry Bonds on steroids.

The specialist's office was in a larger, modernized building, a short drive within the same complex. As the day's designated driver, I had little choice but to accompany my friend, though truth be told, my curiosity was aroused, given how the visit to Dr. Sanjay ended. At this point, I wasn't overly concerned about my friend's well-being, although this was beginning to change; what would not change to any significant degree was John's upbeat attitude.

"I'm here to see Doctor Merriwether," John volunteered.

I noted that the name, followed by "Endocrinologist," was one among many spelled out in little plastic white letters pinned to a large, black felt board. The waiting area was up-sized and expensive-looking—from the plush, cushiony chairs to the color-coordinated murals. An army of workers sat behind a shiny marble counter processing medical bills, which, in all likelihood, were also upsized.

We didn't have to wait long before being called in.

Waiting would come later.

A nurse did the customary preliminary exam and, surprisingly, a lengthy Q&A.

Doctor Merriwether came in. She had not dressed in the standard white coat uniform that automatically raises a patient's blood pressure. Her demeanor was calm, confident, and self-assured. A stethoscope hung loosely around her graceful neck. She glanced at John, then me, and quickly addressed my friend.

"You're John Whitmore."

There was no chance of confusion based on our relative sizes, but intuition must have kicked in when she again faced me and said, "You must be his sidekick."

"I've been hired to protect him."

My remark elicited a smile and a witty reply. "That's very considerate of you ... though I imagine, given his size, you don't see the need arising."

John said nothing and watched the exchange with a grin.

After making her patient feel at ease, Dr. Merriwether quickly got down to business. She was sufficiently prepared, relegating her laptop to the counter behind her and beginning in mid-thought. "As to the weight gain, well, John, any number of things could easily explain that, so we need to focus on the five-centimeter increase in height."

"What are you hoping ... bad word ... expecting to find?" John asked.

"There's a rare disorder called acromegaly that is typically triggered by the pituitary gland producing too much growth hormone. An elevated level of IGF, insulin-like growth factor, would be a good indicator. The problem is that for someone your age, clinical signs of the disease are the lengthening of bones in the hands, feet, and head. Never an overall increase in height."

"Wait a minute. Did you say never? As in, not ever?"

"Never. Growth plates stop doing their thing at about age twenty."

"So I'm forced to buy new clothes and shoes, not knowing if they'll fit a week from now." He smiled, adding, "I'm too old to try out for the Knicks."

"I see your frustration," Merriwether offered. "I will be consulting my colleagues and historical medical records on the possible cause of your condition. We will try our utmost to get to the bottom of this. A growth hormone suppression test is indicated. The unusual nature of your case allows me to expedite results. Before proceeding, check with the billing department to ensure no financial surprises."

"Let the fun begin," John said, expecting the worst.

"You'll find two lovely ladies who will help you there," Merriwether said. Nudging us out the exam room door, she glanced at John and said: "And, F ... Y ... I, I'm a Bulls fan anyway."

Finding the claims department was easy: It occupied the largest room in the facility. Guarding the entrance were two imposing desks separated by a narrow aisle. Behind each desk sat a woman daring anyone to pass.

"You must be Scylla," John said, working off a nameplate that prominently displayed 'Sheryll.'

"My name is pronounced *Sheryll*," said the lady as she gazed up.

"Isn't that what I said?"

"I don't think so."

It took me a moment to catch on—John was remembering his Greek mythology. "Don't mind him," I said, entirely for my friend's amusement. "He's got wax in his ears."

Another blank look from Sheryll.

"Doctor Merriwether requested some additional tests," John said. "I'm here to see if my insurance covers them."

For the fourth time today, John provided identification,

including his name and date of birth.

"The doctor didn't enter a CPT in the system," Sheryll said, annoyed.

"Sorry. CPT?" John asked.

"Current Procedural Terminology," Sheryll said as if the acronym's meaning should have been as evident as the frown on her face.

"Is that important?" John ventured.

Sheryll was not a person to be trifled with. "It's only as important as the difference between obtaining approval for a vasectomy versus that of a hysterectomy. Every medical procedure is coded using one of hundreds of CPT numbers."

"Shall we draw a random number," John asked, "and see if something exciting like 'colonoscopy' comes up?"

While we were busy wasting Sheryll's time, she read out the doctor's order, which was visible on her monitor: "Hormone growth suppression test. Stat. Hmmm. I don't know what somebody told you, but getting authorization will take an hour or more."

"Waiting rooms," I lamented. "Where dreams and the occasional patient go to die."

"Usually, this takes hours and sometimes days."

Eighty minutes later, John was informed that the procedure was authorized. "You're in luck," Sheryll said. "The only 'out-of-pocket' expense will be a copay."

For now, John had sufficient coverage: The physician and facility were 'in network,' the medical tests were covered, and his family's expensive monthly insurance premium, yearly deductible, and per-visit co-pay were all paid—each requirement administered by a healthcare system that has grown too big to be efficient and cost-effective.

The test was scheduled for the following day.

"I guess I am lucky," John said. "Others, not so much. They spend their last dime and file for bankruptcy, or suffer the health consequences of not seeking proper medical treatment."

"Lucky as in surviving Russian Roulette," I replied. "No, *American* Roulette with five bullets in the chamber."

John squeezed into my compact car and adjusted his seat position. "The doc is quite attractive," he said. "Don't you think?"

I agreed.

We sat in silence for a spell.

I wondered if there would come a sorry time when my friend would be unable to drive.

3. NO ANSWERS

FOR NOT ENTIRELY SELFLESS reasons, I volunteered to go with John and Amanda to their follow-up visit at Dr. Merriwether's. I smelled a possible story brewing. I also found myself attracted to the good, as in *very* good, doctor.

The consultation was held in her private office. She was facing the three of us at her desk. Mounted on the wall were several framed degrees and important-looking accolades. Photographs of a personal nature, primarily of her engaged in wilderness hiking, were nearby on a small table. I was grateful to see that none of the photos showed her with anyone resembling a spouse or a significant other. I was more than thankful to see how fit she looked in hiking shorts.

"Nothing helps the immune system like a day in the sun," Merriwether said, noticing my interest in the photographs.

"Is that Lyon Mountain?" I asked, gesturing at one of the photos.

"You've been?" she responded with an appreciative nod.

"Love the view from the fire tower."

Four mugs of coffee appeared from the employee cafeteria.

She was doing her best to make us feel comfortable. The attempt to put us at ease was not working on Amanda, who rightfully believed that bad news was coming. "Would you repeat what you previously told my husband?" she asked, understandably anxious and wasting no time with pleasantries.

"Yes, of course," Merriwether said, then explained why the hormone suppression test was necessary. "And I'm afraid, John, the test came back negative. Neither my colleagues nor I understand the cause of your growth spurt."

"So, you have no clue?" Amanda said, dissatisfied. "Well, if nothing else, you *are* expensive. Tell me, where else can you pay so much and get so little?"

Merriwether flinched at the remark. John and I exchanged surprised glances and braced ourselves for hostilities. No need. Recovering quickly, Merriwether leveled her eyes at Amanda and said, smiling, "I would offer a money-back guarantee, but to tell you the gods' honest truth, I don't believe my colleagues would allow it."

Amanda returned a cordial smile with her own and visibly relaxed. "I like her, John," she said.

I, too, was beginning to like this doctor.

"Where do we go from here?" John inquired.

"If we can't determine the cause of your affliction, we cannot know the future rate of progression. So, more testing. An MRI of your pituitary gland and your knee and elbow joints. Do you have metal implants?"

John pointed at his chest. "Only a heart of gold."

"And a magnetically resonant personality," I added.

Amanda looked at Merriwether and said, "Putting these two together is dangerous. They're always like this. Men. Do they ever grow up?"

"Not in my experience, but if you can put up with them, I can. I've convinced the radiologist to read the images stat."

Another visit to the insurance department was considered

prudent. The three of us were temporarily redirected to the waiting room, allowing Amanda to grill me about my brief exchange with the attractive doctor.

"Today's visit is more of a social call for you, *isn't it?*" she accused. "Shall I get the dope on her?"

I looked at John. "What did you tell her?"

He shrugged. "Facts, simply the facts. Can I help it if she gets a little carried away?"

"A show of my affection," she said. "He needs a little subtle prodding."

"You have the subtlety of a taser," I said.

Sheryll summoned us. Something in her demeanor told us the news wasn't good.

"Name and date of birth," she asked John.

"Same as before, I think."

"Which was?"

"Not sure. Did I use the Islamic, Hebrew, or Julian calendar?"

"The one that allowed me to process your request."

John complied.

"I'm sorry, but the insurance company has denied authorization for the MRI."

"On what grounds?" John asked.

"Not medically necessary."

"That's not a satisfactory answer," Amanda interjected. "Please get whoever you spoke to back on the phone."

"That's not how it works here, Miss," Sheryll began.

"*Mrs.*," Amanda corrected, holding up her wedding band. "On the line. Now, please."

"Yup, it's Mrs.," John confirmed.

"Better off listening to her," I added.

Sheryll stared at the three of us, trying to decide if she was overmatched. Unsure of what to do, she contacted Merriwether, who, over the phone, we heard say: "Make an exception."

The insurance company rep was contacted and told he was on speakerphone with others listening. John's policy number and a brief medical history were repeated. We could hear the background noises of a call center—the plaintive voices of frustrated callers.

"So, who will I have the pleasure of speaking to?" the rep began. I couldn't place the accent, but it wasn't from this hemisphere.

"I'm John Whitmore. With me is my wife, Amanda. She speaks for me."

"And may I have your name, please?" Amanda asked the rep.

"Scott Griffin."

I held my tongue regarding the irony. In mythology, griffins were guardians of the king's treasure.

"So, you're denying coverage," Amanda said, "despite the thousands we pay in monthly premiums."

"That is correct," Griffin answered. "For services to be covered, they must be considered medically necessary, as determined by a diagnosis. There is no diagnosis. In addition, an ailment has to be treatable. No doctor is suggesting a way to stop Mr. Whitmore from growing, let alone *reducing* his height and weight. We don't consider making people shorter medically necessary."

After several minutes of back-and-forth, explanations, and protests, Amanda could tolerate no more.

"Let me ask you a question, Mr. Griffin," she said. "Have you read Vonnegut?"

"Uh ... yes, but ..."

"So, follow along. Because acromegaly has been ruled out, and there is no diagnosis, additional testing is not covered. But my husband's problem can't be diagnosed *without* further testing. Doesn't that sound like a 'Catch-22' to you, Mr. Griffin?"

"That is my company's decision, ma'am. It would be best if you understood your policy restrictions. Beyond that, my advice is that you appeal our decision. I should tell you that the appeal process can take as long as two months."

"Two months!" Amanda repeated. "I won't insult you by stating the obvious."

It was obvious and upsetting to me that it meant terrible medical and financial news for my friend and his family.

We returned to the waiting room and, after a mercifully brief wait, were escorted to Dr. Merriwether's office. Terminating a call, she had a frown on her face. "I tried but couldn't sway them. However, I consulted this practice's medical director concerning our fees. In turn, he contacted the corporation's financial director. This facility will absorb a portion of the MRI and certain other charges if John agrees to pay the balance."

It would be the first payment of many that would be highly detrimental to the Whitmores' finances. Later, with a sense of humor somehow intact, John said it best: "They each manage to take their pound of flesh, but somehow I still keep growing."

John and Amanda expressed thanks for the effort made on their behalf. The in-house MRI was performed, and the results were sent to Dr. Merriwether's computer. We watched her eyes widen as she read the radiologist's report and examined the relevant images. Shaking her head, she called and spoke to the technician in charge, asking if some error had been made. Not quite satisfied with the response, she contacted the radiologist.

"I knew you'd call me," he began.

"I have the patient here. Did you ..."

"Reach out to the tech? Oh yeah. But only to find out if he was somehow—God knows how—pranking me. I was going to ream him a new one."

"The last line in your report ... 'Patient is getting bigger.' Really? That's your medical opinion?"

"In comparison to a scan the patient had from five years ago. Look here, you're the diagnostician. Did you ask the patient if he fell in a vat of Miracle-Grow?"

"Jesus, Bob!"

"Sorry, Jessica. Forgot I was on speaker."

The call ended on that note.

"I can't apologize enough for that," Merriwether said. "He rarely sees patients."

"Not a problem," John said. "I'd be upset if it weren't amusing."

"His report defies explanation. You're not only getting taller but proportionately bigger. Every bone has increased in size. At a minimum, this would require viable bone growth plates at the knee and elbow. Given your age, that in itself would be quite extraordinary. The MRI has ruled this out."

"Isn't that good news?" Amanda asked.

"Not necessarily. We are left with a greater mystery: In what manner are bones growing? We eliminated one remote possibility, acromegaly, leaving nothing to point to a diagnosis."

"What do we do now?" John asked.

Under our stare, Merriwether considered the question.

"The uniqueness of your condition ... I'm at a loss for the right term ... leads me to believe that the best course of action is to refer you to a local research hospital. They have extensive experience in the diagnosis and treatment of rare diseases, and their departments specialize in genetics and cellular biology. They will review the medical record to determine your acceptance as a patient."

The suggestion provided a glimmer of hope. Maybe it shouldn't have, but on this day, John weighed 185 pounds and was six feet two and one-half inches tall. No one imagined just how big he would get. Human imagination has its limits, dictated by the laws of nature and experience.

As we rose to leave, Amanda, acting in character, nudged John: "I think Max has a sensitive personal question for the doctor. We wouldn't want to intrude on his privacy, *would we*?" She pushed her spouse outside the doctor's office door, leaving me standing there. Awkwardly.

"I like her," Merriwether said, referring to Amanda and giving me time to recover my composure.

"So do I," I responded. "I also like eating habanero peppers and standing outside to watch lightning storms."

"I appreciate a good sense of humor."

"Same. It appears we have something else in common," I said, making a point of looking at the openly displayed photographs.

She leaned back in her chair and waited. Being accomplished, assured, and attractive, she wouldn't make whatever I had in mind too easy. I would have to manage this 'old school.' 'Come here often?' wouldn't exactly work.

"I'm trying to say I'd like to get to know you better."

"Your friends certainly seem to endorse that idea. Please call me Jessica."

"Jessica," I acknowledged. "I've known John a long time. Amanda, too."

"He seems to be coping exceptionally well."

"That he is. By conscious choice."

"I'm very sorry I couldn't help him."

"I'm sure he and Amanda know that."

An aide poked her head into the open doorway, did a quick double-take, smiled, and backed out. She wanted the doctor to know that poor souls were waiting, lost in limbo in the waiting room.

"I shouldn't take too much of your time," I said. "Exchange cell numbers?"

"Give me yours. I'll text you."

And so I did.

Back at the car, Amanda was waiting to ambush me.

"And?"

"Could you try," I said, deliberately delaying an answer, "to at least take the time to form a complete sentence? Maybe use a noun and a verb?"

"How's this? Did you ask her out, shithead?"

"Much better."

"And?"

"It's all Gucci."

"Truth?"

"Truth."

"Awesome!"

Later, after a somber reality had set in, Amanda focused her attention on John, with me only getting hit by shrapnel.

"I know you're taking what's happening seriously. You better be! You *both* better be!"

"I always listen to your advice, sweetheart," John said. "But think how strange this all is. How strange life can be. If life gives you lemons, make lemonade. So they say. But why not add bourbon, ginger ale, and some sprigs of mint?"

Amanda hugged him. If more was discussed, it wasn't in my presence.

That was the closest they had to an argument, which was no argument at all.

"Sorry, you're getting some bad news," I finally managed.

"I have little choice in the matter," my friend said. "I either roll with this, or it rolls over me."

I felt guilty about what I was about to propose (at the time, the Whitmores' finances weren't in dire straits like mine), for it had more to do with me helping my languishing writing career. "I have an idea that might benefit us both. Why not allow me to record all that goes on with you?"

"Or up?" John said. "My head out a moonroof like Geoffrey the Giraffe?"

Misplaced humor? Not in our eyes. That's how it was with John and me.

"Only with your final say."

"Keep talking."

"I would need access to you most of the time. My presence may get intrusive. Can you tolerate my company for as long as necessary?"

"That street runs in both directions, doesn't it, bro?"

"Hey, if things get crazy-strange, there may be some real coin in this. Split 50-50 on the story rights? Assuming there'll be one."

"Sounds fair to me. I do the growing, and you do the writing."

So, we agreed. Not having polished my crystal ball, I had no clue that I would be a witness to the absurd. My motive may have been as pure as NYC snow, but if my friend was to face his burden with a sense of humor, then who better than me to share it with?

4. DOLPHINS ON THE CEILING

JOHN'S ADMISSION INTO THE research hospital was delayed because a portion of the facility's doctoral staff had convinced themselves that the medical record submitted for review was a prank to undermine their good standing. Who could blame them for their skepticism? When these fears were (mostly) allayed, a protracted battle ensued over who would have the privilege of being the hospital's admitting physician. After all, the case's uniqueness did present a serious opportunity to enhance one's reputation.

So, having received no word concerning his application, and in the absence of a diagnosis, John and I turned to the internet for answers. Not blind to the pitfalls of doing so, we were not taking our efforts too seriously. In short order, surfing sent us down the rabbit hole of "alternative" medicine, specifically the discipline of holistic well-being, where we found as many advocates as critics.

Our education continued on a sweltering spring afternoon as we sipped decaf in a coffee shop peopled by Gen-Zers listening to podcasts or "working" from home. Nobody made eye contact. That didn't bother me much. What could that lead to? Conversation?

I sat directly across from John, his long legs accidentally kicking me under the table. He was now six-five and weighed one-ninety-five—not yet big enough to garner undue attention. That would come.

"I've searched for anything even remotely similar to what is going on with me," my friend said. "As it turns out, I am not alone. In Russia, a comrade called Zherdyaj is tall enough to warm his hands on chimney tops. At night, he scares the crap out of little kids."

"A useful skill."

"Closer to home," John continued, "there's a fifteen-foot chap called Slender Man who skulks about in forests and abducts little children. Dressed in a suit and tie."

"It's important to make a good impression."

"I did get a little sidetracked. Unfortunately, I found nothing useful, and with all the surfing came an onslaught of pesky pop-up ads."

"Like what?"

"Clothing for big and tall men. Custom, oversized beds, big office chairs, and the like. Items I never knew existed. Did you know that they make extra-long golf clubs? When I researched alternative medicine, strange shit appeared, like diets claiming to increase height. I came across professionals with bona fide degrees. Others were suspect. Probably quacks."

"You know 'quack' comes from a Dutch term 'quacksalver,' someone who cures using home remedies."

"How in the hell do you know that?"

"Research for a magazine piece I wrote."

"That's helpful ... if it ever comes up in *Trivial Pursuit*. So, now

I'm flooded with texts and emails from alternative and holistic places. I block them or send them to spam, except one that's pissing me off. My personal touch seems to be required. They're local, so I've scheduled an appointment. Care to visit the place?"

"I wouldn't miss it."

We finished our coffees and headed out onto the crowded roads. I've found that the type and model of vehicles observed, along with their drivers, reflect society. Meaning it tested my patience. We passed a 40-ish male behind the wheel of a beat-up Corolla with the license plate 'GAVE UP.' Soon afterward, we spotted a Tesla Model S Plaid with a gold-rimmed vanity plate, '0PTI0NS,' with the numerical '0' substituted for the letters 'O.' The driver, a fifty-ish male dressed in a suit and tie, was texting as he sped past us on the right shoulder. Unlike John, I don't take this kind of rude behavior well. That he might be a wealthy options trader (which often meant betting on a company cratering) contributed to my salty mood.

"Evolution gave us five fingers," I said, "so we can give arrogant pricks like that the middle one."

"All this time," John said, "I thought it was the use of an opposable thumb. Anyway, chill. The guy is probably heading to Wall Street. I'd wager his limo driver quit. The guy with the 'GAVE UP' plates."

"Tough life," I said, still angry. "Not being able to copter in from the Hamptons."

"Life's too short. Why be overly concerned about it? You gain nothing."

We turned off the main road and headed away from the business district. "Is that the facility over there?" I pointed to an imposing three-story Victorian house girded with manicured evergreens that looked like a pack of over-groomed poodles instead of naturally growing vegetation.

Walking up the entry path, we were treated to the soft tinkling of wind chimes hanging from the front porch's overhanging soffit.

"I'm going to enjoy this," John said with a mischievous grin.
"Shall I participate?"

"That, my friend, goes without saying."

Inside, the smell of incense failed, as always, to mask the pungent scent of cannabis. Our eyes were drawn to the shimmering cascade of a ceiling-to-floor wall fountain. "Good feng shui," John commented.

"What do you know about feng shui?" I asked.

"Absolutely nothing."

There was greenery in the form of yellow-flowered bromeliads, waxy-leafed rubber trees, and several species of veg I could not identify. A small sign hung nearby stating, "PLEASE CONVERSE WITH OUR PLANTS."

"What troubles me greatly," I commented, "is that the word 'converse' implies some form of dialogue. A back-and-forth, a tête-à-tête, if you will. I'm out of my depth here. Exactly what could you talk about?"

"Horticulturally?" John said, stroking a tender leaf. "Certainly nothing concerning that beautiful weather we're having outside."

With visions of *Little Shop of Horrors*, I politely addressed one of the loquacious shrubberies. "Greetings, my perennial friend. Let me introduce my bro here. He's a devout vegetarian."

"It's a lie!" John protested, suddenly backing away.

Our antics woke a lithe, elderly lady who emerged from the pervasive ether to stand behind the front counter. John introduced me while confirming his appointment.

"Please take a seat and fill out these forms," Mabel said. I didn't know her name. She looked like a Mabel.

"I may not stay long," John replied.

"Oh?" Mabel replied, appearing confused. "Well, you must fill 'em out to see the practitioner."

"And what type of practitioner would I be seeing?" John questioned. "Your website gave the impression that a medical professional was on staff."

Mabel responded with a shrug. We abandoned her and took a seat.

A framed document hung on the wall: *Bachelor of Alternative Medicine*. I googled that there was some merit in the proper application of the degree. Still, it was not unusual for 'bad actors' to operate beyond the boundary of their learning, mucking it up for everyone else. The facility's practitioner, Gasper K. Stubin, had obtained his degree online from a little-known college. I shared what I found with John, but he knew most of it, and another nugget I learned later.

Ornate glass tables bookended the cushiony couch we sat on. One held fuzzy, colorful neoprene balls that you repeatedly squeeze to alleviate tension and stifle the urge to punch people like OPTIONS' lights out. A heavy, cut-crystal bowl of hard candy squatted on the other table. I freed a reluctant mint from its wrapper. "This pleasure parlor," I observed, popping the mint in my mouth, "has all the senses covered: Sight, sound, smell, touch, and finally, taste."

"That's only five," John commented. "There are probably others lurking here somewhere."

"No cap," I said, grinning.

One of the forms was an extensive questionnaire. The first inquiry (occupying a good chunk of real estate at the top of the page) was a gender inquiry, followed by forty-two possible answers, not counting the fill-in-the-blank option.

Although John and I couldn't give a damn about a person's orientation, our 'woke' attitude in no way precluded us, as with all things, from savaging the topic in any and all ways possible.

"What were they thinking, printing this?" John complained. "The question is monumentally outdated. There are far more than forty-two orientations. Last I looked, *Facebook* mentions fifty-eight."

"Do you see yourself on the list?"

"'Male' isn't listed. The closest would be 'cis male.' I'll have to write in one of my own." He took a moment to reflect. "Got it. 'Stud muffin.'"

I almost choked on my mint.

"There's a question about income. Very inappropriate." I watched as John wrote in 'Not Nearly Enough.'

Meanwhile, a disheveled young man, avoiding eye contact, walked in and slumped into a corner armchair. Mabel curtly said, "Go in," and he disappeared into an adjoining room. A minute later, he emerged, handed her something that may have been money, and left. Curious, I thought.

"Help me with some of these entries," John, who also had been watching, asked, "'Which way is your front door facing?'"

There are a few hundred million people who believe in feng shui. John and I weren't among them. "I'd go with 'Timbuktu,'" I offered.

"Multiple choice," John continued, reading aloud: "'Marijuana Use: 1x month, 1x week, 1x day, more than 1x per day?'"

"You're saying 'None' is not a choice?"

"No."

While my friend was completing the form, I distracted myself by reading the pamphlets on the adjoining table. "Here's something for you to digest—pardon the pun: *Urine Health Tonic. Proven Health Benefits of Drinking Your Urine.*"

"Served neat or on ice?"

"On the rocks. Kidney stones."

"I'm dead," John said, laughing.

A tall, thin, graying middle-aged man with spectacles wafted in like an apparition, the illusion partly dispelled when the beaded curtain he passed through obeyed the laws of physics and moved aside.

"Hello ... uhm, gentlemen?" said Gasper K. Stubin, questioning my presence.

"A friend of mine," John said. "For comfort."

"Like a soothing cup of tea or a soft blankie," I added.

"Please follow me."

Stubin guided us down a confusing maze of narrow passageways. The scent of incense and weed increased as we neared the inner sanctum. We passed a darkened room with a slightly ajar door that was rapidly closed. John was able to get a quick look inside. "I think I'm experiencing a contact high," my friend whispered. "I could swear I just saw someone lying on their back staring at images of dolphins frolicking on the ceiling."

"Nothing would surprise me here," I said. "Or should I say *everything* would?"

There were several other small rooms we would never get to see. The room we entered was relatively empty. My initial assessment of Stubin was beginning to solidify when I spied a jar labeled 'Sativa' on a nearby counter. The surface was bare except for a blood pressure cuff still in its original packaging. I doubted Stubin knew how to use it. "Your answers are a bit unorthodox," the man remarked, referencing the questionnaire.

"How is 'what is your annual income?' relevant to anything?" John asked.

"In two ways, my friend. A wealthy person, unlike a poor one, has a different lifestyle and mindset. Therefore, he has different psychosomatic needs that must be addressed. Perhaps, uh, alternative treatment modalities would be indicated."

Like how much to overcharge, I thought to myself. I detected the odor of bullshit, unmasked by incense. Stubin continued to read John's handiwork. "None of these questions, uh," he said, chuckling, "have serious responses. I gather you don't see the need to properly fill this out?"

"I took some liberties," John said.

"A height gain, you entered, of five inches, uh, in weeks?! Very amusing."

"That one was serious."

"Not possible."

"Let's say it is. What would you recommend?"

"Now we're getting somewhere," Stubin said. "It would be best if you had asked earlier. Would you prefer edible or smokable?"

"Not interested," John said.

"So, why did you come here?"

"At first, just to get you to stop pestering me with texts and emails."

Stubin's face flushed red. "That's the only reason you came here? To waste my time?"

"I see it quite differently. It is you who wasted mine."

An imposing man entered from a side door. "Problem here?" he mouthed, addressing Stubin but glaring menacingly at John.

For as long as I have known him, John has preferred to avoid physical confrontations. He stood to face the large man. "Nice of you to show us out. No telling what would happen if we wandered lost in here."

As we left, John added, "Stop sending me nonsense, Stubin. You don't want me back for a second visit." Then I found out what else my friend knew, which I didn't. "And by the way, in this state, a license to dispense cannabis is required and must be prominently displayed."

The implication of what John might do with this knowledge—and our visit—had the desired effect. He immediately stopped receiving texts and emails.

5. FIVE HUNDRED POUND GORILLA

I WAS SITTING AT John and Amanda's kitchen table, the three of us enjoying breakfast, the inviting smell of sizzling bacon, rather than weed, permeating the air.

Bacon, unfortunately, was not the only thing being grilled.

"Where are the kids?" I asked, attempting to change the conversation, as the topic was my first non-date with Jessica, A.K.A. Doctor Merriwether. I cared very much about my friends' two children, for I had known them since their birth and enjoyed their company.

"I believe," Amanda persisted, addressing John, keeping one eye on me, "that the expression is 'punching above your weight.' Would you like more OJ?"

"I don't want to finish it all," John replied. He poured himself a third glass. "Max's not worried about Jessica being better looking than him ..."

"...or smarter," Amanda added.

"Right. Or smarter. He's used to that. Almost everybody is."

John was doing his utmost to keep the mood upbeat despite

growing to six feet seven inches and two hundred eighteen pounds. I noticed he had consumed an omelet of four eggs, bacon enough to create two tic-tac-toe grids, and four thick slices of multigrain toast. I don't think he intended to finish the loaf.

"Listen, Max," Amanda said. "If John's private life is fair game, then yours is, too."

"There's not much to tell," I said, succumbing to the badgering. "We texted. That's it."

"No Netflix and chill?"

"Don't get yourself too excited now."

"Can't be helped," Amanda replied. "You're in uncharted territory, not meeting through a dating app."

"Max knows where Jessica works," John said. "It's more difficult for her to ghost him ... not that she would want to," he quickly added.

"Your vote of confidence," I clapped back, "means a lot to me."

In a convoluted way, it did. We were fam—permission in perpetuity granted to bust balls.

Brad, their older child, entered the room and grabbed a slice of bacon off his dad's plate. He did not intend to stay, so I had fun slowing him down with the rapid-fire round of the three questions kids hate.

"How's school? Dating anyone? What do you wanna be when you grow up?"

"SMH."

"Don't know that one."

"Everyone knows 'shaking my head.'"

Like most young boys, Brad was a smart ass. He expected me to tease him, so I did.

"Off to soccer, I see. You know it's called football in the rest of the world?"

"*Everyone* knows that, too."

An endearing quality of a pre-teen is how easily they insult others. Hey, I was asking for it.

"Remember, you can't use your hands!" I shouted to his back as he rocketed out the front door.

"Interesting choice, making me his godfather," I remarked to the parents. And so I am—his godfather, minus the religious underpinnings.

Parents have their work cut out for them, raising kids in suburbia. Socializing activities are usually miles away and car-dependent, leaving neighborhoods empty. Children have fewer opportunities to interact and play outdoors independently of adults. Cell phones and computers exert too big an influence.

Making sense of the new social norms can be challenging as you get on in years. An example comes to mind. "Why, in God's name," my mom once innocently asked, "would a teenage boy send a picture of his junk to a girl?" I refrained from laughing and directed her to the Urban Dictionary.

"John," I said, "how do your kids feel about what's happening to you?"

He pushed back his empty plate and took a few moments to consider. "Well, you should know that what they say is never just one thing, and as a parent, you learn that what they *say* is not necessarily what they *feel*. On occasion, Brad jokes about it ..."

"...just like his father," Amanda chimed in.

"He likes to say," John continued, "that I'm morphing into some new type of superhero. Our daughter is alternately embarrassed, amazed, and confused. She also worries about being teased if her dad goes viral."

Amanda amplified: "They both have defense mechanisms for coping."

As we continued talking, Carrie, a slender girl much younger than her brother, came up behind her father and draped her hands around his neck. I wondered if she sensed a time when that simple act of affection would become physically impossible.

"Hi, Max," Carrie said. I can't remember when I last heard a kid call an adult by their last name. The days of saying 'mister' or 'ma'am' are gone. I have no issue with that, but my parents do.

"What's up, darling?"

"Mom says you have a bae."

"I said he *might* have," Amanda protested.

"I'm jealous." There was truth to her feelings. As her dad's best friend, she had known me her entire life. "When can I meet her? She better be bussin."

"Well, uh ... Settle for 'fire?' I'm sure she'd love you."

"Honey, sit down and eat breakfast," John said.

"I ate already, Dad. Vibing with Jennie today."

"I want you home for lunch."

The young girl's charm and sweetness caused me to ponder why I hadn't gone down the path of marriage and kids. My shaky personal finances? Was I too immature? Too self-absorbed? Afraid of responsibility? Like many people my age, I did not want to make the required sacrifices. I never bought into the excuse 'the right woman hasn't come along' for it implied that one day I'd hear a knock on the door, and poof! The woman of my dreams would be magically standing there.

With both children out of the home, Amanda took the opportunity to let me in on some bad news:

"Got laid off."

"No shit? Really?" Given the recent strain on their finances, the news was disturbing.

"Seems pretty real to me," she said, frowning. "I was given two weeks' notice—with no severance pay. My boss is a dick. When asked why I was fired, he regurgitated BS about the payroll being too big and that companies, to survive, have little choice but to 'downsize' in today's economy."

'Downsizing.' Wall Street embraces the term. Sounds less

draconian than 'getting the axe.' Amanda's termination, I suspected, had more to do with taking unscheduled leave from work to be with her husband during doctor visits. She left that part unsaid, at least to me, though John would have suspected as much. Neither spouse wanted the other to feel bad.

"Are you guys going to be alright?" I asked, knowing that John's medical bills could significantly drain their family finances.

"Things will work out," John said.

"I'll find work," Amanda said, sidestepping the inquiry.

"You have to appreciate the irony, Max," John offered. "Amanda's a victim of down-sizing; I'm a victim of up-sizing. Admission into the research hospital is still a work in progress, but I should hear from them soon."

"And driving?" I asked.

"If I outgrow my Santa Fe, I can rent a larger SUV. Something with an impressive-sounding name like Yukon, Armada, or Battlestar Galactica."

If he became too big, what then? Recline in the back of an RV and let someone else drive?

On another unseasonably warm early evening, Jessica and I found ourselves at the Whitmores'. One of their home's best features is a spacious deck constructed with an 'ethically sourced,' incredibly dense wood called IPE that could outlast the supporting structure beneath. Without warning, a perfect-looking deck could collapse from too much snow or people. Or John's weight alone if he continued to expand at the current rate.

Until then, the deck overlooked a small Koi pond and a colorful garden bursting with flowering perennials. Mosquitoes or yellowjackets, the plague of outdoor suburban dining, were absent. We would seize the opportunity to imbibe cocktails and wine to our hearts' content and our livers' discontent. We had arrived and would depart using ride-share.

Before our adult party began in earnest, Carrie fulfilled her wish to meet Jessica, whom she considered the rival for my affection. They quickly hit it off, with our hosts gleefully watching as the two of them went back and forth, ending with:

"So, are you or are you not gonna be Max's new girlfriend?"

"Have you asked Max that question?" Jessica replied.

(Clever, I thought, putting me in the hot seat.)

"Maxie," Carrie prodded, "is Jessica your bae?"

"She's a friend. Will you settle for 'bestie' for now?"

"Tell me!"

I wasn't sure how to answer. "Well ...," I began.

Thankfully, Amanda stepped in. "This is too painful to watch," she said, rescuing me by gently grabbing her reluctant daughter by the elbow and ushering her to the front door, where parents had arrived to whisk the young girl away to a sleepover.   The invitation was not for dinner. Instead, there was a large charcuterie board filled with premium meats, a variety of delectable cheeses, pâté, fig jam, pistachios, grapes, sun-dried tomatoes, and other delicacies I could not name but thoroughly enjoyed all the same. A basket brimming with specialty bread and crackers completed the picture.

A round of mojitos garnished with fresh mint was served, followed by chilled wine. As the adult beverages began to impart their pleasant effect, I could not help but notice that the attractive ladies, dressed for a sultry evening, had a lot of skin showing. John did, too, thanks to his ample size. On that score, he kept me updated. I was shocked to learn he weighed two hundred forty pounds and stood six feet ten, now tilting his head as he passed through doorways.

"If this is part of your Mediterranean diet, sign me up," I told him, pausing to devour an Italian delicacy.

"You have a lovely home," Jessica commented.

"Thank you," Amanda said. "It's a fair share of work. When the kids are grown, I wonder if it'll be too big for John and me."

"A bit too small right now," John said, pointing to a small

bruise on his forehead. "Brad and Amanda are taking bets on which will come first, either I knock myself unconscious or start remembering to duck."

"I'll take some of that action," Jessica said. "Do you keep smelling salts in the house?"

John laughed the hardest, saying, "One has to appreciate when being maligned is accompanied by good advice."

"Sorry about that," Jessica said, smiling. "It's the wine talking."

"I'm a glass or two away from it shouting," I said.

John uncorked another bottle, a second, or a third, for no one was keeping count. We were drinking excessively, behaving like we could live and act this way forever, precisely because we knew we couldn't. At the time, and I believe he was acutely aware of this, John was the epicenter of our little group of four.   Our Squad.

"Would you like to hear," he began, "some peculiar interactions I've had with my coworkers?"

Our curiosity was aroused, especially mine, for his work life was an aspect of John's evolving story from which I had been excluded.

"Initially," my friend began, "comments from the men were about my weight. Remarks such as 'John, have you been hitting the gym?' Or, 'Better lay off the rhoids.'"

"Sounds like something men would say," Amanda said dismissively.

"I don't want to humblebrag, but the women had a different take," John responded. "I believe more than a few of the younger women expressed appreciation of my size."

"Better not tell me who they are," Amanda warned. "For their sake."

"I've got your back, girlfriend," Jessica added. "I have access to drugs ... if you happen to need them."

"Be warned, John," I said. "They're already conspiring together."

Refilling our glasses, he continued:

"How people reacted was a progression of sorts. The first inch added to my height was harder for people to process. There were double-takes but few comments. They felt something was different about me, but what? Another few days, another inch, and the comments were about everything *but* my height. 'Did you change your hairstyle?' for example. My secretary finally said, 'You're wearing platform shoes, right? If not, either you're somehow getting taller, or I'm getting shorter.'"

"How'd you answer?" Jessica asked.

"Told the truth, 'I'm growing.' And you know, not one person in the office, except possibly my secretary, believed me. Not initially. They assumed I was joking. But humor is something I can relate to. I called the office staff Lilliputians, warning them not to piss me off. To their credit, a few coworkers laughed, grokking the reference from *Gulliver's Travels*."

Judging by their confused expressions, Jessica and Amanda didn't grok. So, I volunteered to explain. "Gulliver drank too much. Let's say he was over-hydrated, then found a *very* personal way of putting out a palace fire."

"You'll have to excuse these two," Amanda advised. "Wine or no, this is how they act."

"If you're worried about them offending or shocking me, don't be," Jessica replied. "I *am* a doctor, you know."

Amanda was ready to put it to the test. Referring to Jessica and me, she came out with: "When's the last time either of you had sex?"

Jessica colored slightly, but not I, having learned from experience what Amanda was capable of.

"For me?" I responded. "Pleistocene Epoch. Might have been longer. Should we do it for the plot?"

"It's been a while," Jessica admitted. Recovering quickly, she added, "Why? Have I lost a contest?"

"Just a little concerned," Amanda replied. "If you don't use it, you lose it."

"That's my wife," John commented, smirking. "Always watching out for a person's best interest."

"I just see a fabulous opportunity here," Amanda continued.

"*Here*?" I teased. "Right now?"

"Clear the table!" Jessica suggested, making a motion to rise.

"No, you idiots."

Silliness ruled the night. I was gratified to see Jessica fit right in. There was only one rule, which was unwritten: Avoid talking about the five-hundred-pound gorilla in the room.

What if John never stopped growing?

When it was nearly time to leave, I grabbed my cell and arranged the ride-share. Curious, I asked John, "How many bottles did we drink?"

"Five or six, I think," he said. "Sleep here. Jessica, too. We could open the forty-year-old port."

I shook my head to indicate 'no.' I heard Jessica talking and laughing with Amanda.

"I'd offer to drive you both home or wherever, but it's not a good idea, my driving. I'm not above the law, you know. Not yet, anyway." On the way to the front door, the top of John's head greeted the top of the hallway door frame in a less-than-friendly way. "Way too much to drink," he said. "That one doesn't count for shit."

Jessica and I lived five miles apart. Everywhere in suburbia seems five miles apart. Her apartment was the first stop.

"I had a great time," she said. "I'd invite you in, and this is a hell of a time to be sensible, but I'm pretty lit."

"Same," I said, seeing her to her door.

"Maybe next time," she said, kissing me goodnight.

Arriving home, I lay on my bed and stared at the slowly spinning ceiling.

Thankfully, no dolphins.

6. STYMIED

JOHN WHITMORE WAS ONE screening interview away from admission into the medical maze known as County Central Hospital. Guarding the labyrinth was someone named Dryden, half doctor and half administrator. A healthy percentage of his peers thought him a complete ass.

As with many modern hospitals, CCH was overcrowded and understaffed. It was also too big, overwhelmed by the sheer number of its departments, each a fiefdom in its own right. (From Admissions to Discharge, a large hospital may have three dozen departments or more.) John managed to survive CCH due to the intervention of Dr. Merriwether, who had volunteered to be his patient advocate. The arrangement was advantageous; she knew how to cope with a hospital's system and hierarchy, had a growing personal relationship with the patient, and had extensive medical knowledge. She also had a professional interest in the case.

An advocate may interpret and question diagnoses, ensure

proper and timely treatment, and protect the patient's rights. These responsibilities were made more difficult because Dr. Dryden took exception whenever his directives were questioned. In Dr. Merriwether, however, he was matched by someone exceptionally well-qualified and willing to intercede on John's behalf.

The Squad was kept waiting in Dryden's well-appointed, five-hundred-square-foot office. By comparison, other hospital areas had a tired appearance from constant hard use. The Administrator stood in the doorway, acting friendly with a young secretary. Jessica frowned at his demeanor, then turned her attention to the diplomas and honors hanging on the wall. I was beginning to know her better and concluded she was not overly impressed by what she saw.

Dryden broke off his chatting and walked past us to sit behind his substantial teak desk. My first impression of the man was unfavorable. I've said you don't judge a book by its cover, but the man's arrogance began telling the story. His opening line helped to validate my negative opinion.

"I see that you have a small entourage in tow, Mr. Whitmore."

"I'd hardly call it that," John said. "This is my wife, Amanda, my close friend and confidant, Max, and Doctor Merriwether, acting as my advocate."

Dryden cocked an eye, his attention immediately drawn to Jessica when he heard 'doctor' and 'advocate' — two words he would rather not see together. Before he could ask, she slid a sheet of paper across the expanse of wood in front of her and said: "A signed and notarized document stating that Mr. Whitmore has authorized me to act on his behalf. When he is accepted as a patient, of course."

Dryden ignored the form. "We at Central found the patient's medical history hard to accept, thinking the file submitted to this hospital had mistakes, as they so often do."

"I can assure you there have been no errors," Jessica said. "And the photographic evidence alone, images of John before and after ..."

"Yes, yes," Dryden said dismissively, "photos, of course, can

48

be easily altered by AI. The point I'm making is that it took a lot of convincing, and once our physicians were convinced, let's say there was much internal discussion concerning how to proceed."

I bet, I thought to myself. Having grown to seven feet tall and two hundred fifty pounds, John was a one-of-a-kind medical miracle. Fortunately, except for a small but growing circle of doctors, family members, and co-workers, he had yet to attract undue outside attention. The researchers and physicians at CCH knew that John's relative obscurity was likely to change. They were anxious to get their latex-covered hands on a headline-grabbing patient.

"Seeing John in person does cement our decision," Dryden continued. "It is in everyone's best interest that he be admitted as an inpatient for study."

"'Study?'" Amanda said, anger in her voice. "I don't like the sound of that."

"I, too, am troubled," Jessica said, looking steadily at Dryden, "about the use of that word."

"You have better?" Dryden asked.

"A few," Jessica said. "'Examination.' 'Care.' 'Evaluation.'"

"We are, as you well know," Dryden countered, "the best research hospital within hundreds of miles."

"You are about to accept into your care the most interesting patient on the planet. Your medical curiosity is understandable, but we want assurances that he will be treated in a manner that keeps his health and privacy foremost, not as some research project."

"Of course, of course," Dryden assured. "A patient's medical record is kept secure in *this* hospital. What happens outside of this facility is beyond our control."

Small comfort, I thought. Although HIPAA mandates the protection of patient records, I had trouble believing Dryden wanted to keep a lid on what was happening to my friend.

"'Inpatient,'" Jessica said, reiterating Dryden's word for clarity, "would mean John remains in the hospital overnight. How long?"

"Yes," Dryden said, "for several days, possibly longer."

"That sounds more like 'incarceration' than inpatient," Amanda complained.

"So, exactly what are your feelings about this, John?" Jessica asked.

"I have no desire to be separated from my wife, my kids, or my work."

"Nor I from my husband," Amanda added. "Don't even think it."

"Then it's settled," Jessica said, leaving no room for debate. "John wishes to be accepted on an outpatient basis."

"That would not be a sound decision, Dr. Merriwether," Dryden responded, reddening. "And you know it."

"What I do know," Jessica replied, "is that a person's psychological well-being is as important as their physical. The two aspects shouldn't be separated. If there are good reasons for John to remain in the hospital overnight, make us aware of *what* they are *when* they occur, and he shall be willing to accommodate you."

And so, the issue was decided. The doctors and research assistants who were to be involved were then summoned. What followed was a series of lengthy discussions about treatment and research protocols. Some concepts, those theoretical and highly technical, the Squad did not entirely grasp. Correction: Jessica did— and that would suffice.

John started a series of daily visits to CCH, scheduled to accommodate his working hours. There were occasions, however, when he was directed to remain overnight. Despite the hospital's unintentional attempts to make it otherwise, I always found him in good spirits. On one visit, I found my friend in a hospital gown, backside to me, staring pensively out a window. Mercifully, he turned to face me.

"They keeping you busy?" I asked.

"In a manner. Mostly by asking, and I mean this literally, hundreds of questions, some bordering on the ridiculous."

"'Ridiculous' is relative coming from a man whose ample ass is sticking out the back of a tight hospital gown."

"The nurses don't seem to mind. They claim they couldn't find my size, but I'm starting to grow suspicious."

"Male or female nurses?"

"From what I can tell, both."

Our conversation was interrupted when a man in street clothes peered into the room, stared at John, and hurried away. Similar occurrences took place during my brief stay. "What's up with that?" I asked.

"I'm the object of attention," John answered. "A curiosity. It's only a matter of time before word gets out."

I agreed. "So, what are the absurd questions?"

"'Have you ever used Rogaine?' I don't, of course."

"What's the thought behind the question?"

"Rogaine, besides growing hair, can add on a pound or two. I think the nature of the question points to the doctors' and researchers' desperation."

"Did they ask about Viagra? It's been known to enlarge things."

"No. Not yet. I'll answer 'yes' to see how the nurses react."

"What else did they ask?"

"Did I have contact with unusual or exotic animal species such as bats or primates? Have I consumed bushmeat? Perhaps the best of all: have I had sex with a primate or any other animal?"

"Did you tell them about Bongo the Chimp? That day, you almost quit your job to join the circus?"

"Her *name* was Bonzo," John insisted. "But I'm trying to block all that."

"Again, what are they hoping to find out?"

"An unknown virus that could trigger cell growth and division.

It's just one of several theories they're working on."

"You can just as easily answer questions from home. So why are they keeping you here?"

"They have something more sinister in store for me. Taking cell samples using CT-guided needle biopsies. I'm to be a human pincushion of sorts. I keep thinking of Pinhead from the movie *Hellraiser.* Jessica warned me that it would not be a pleasant experience."

During the remainder of my visit, we were interrupted by Admissions, Human Resources, Diagnostic Imaging, Finance, and Orthopedics staff. An attractive nurse entered to disconnect John's blood pressure and heart rate monitors. She stole a glimpse of his ass. Leaving, she exchanged wry grins with a second nurse entering to take a blood sample. When an aide rushed in and asked what he wanted for dinner, John answered, "Something delicious." We all laughed at the impossibility.

The attending physician arrived. Unlike Dryden, he was personable. "Hello, *Doctor Zhivago,*" he said, addressing me. I had signed the visitor log to amuse my juvenile self, believing no one would notice.

"How'd you know it was me?" I asked.

"The aide staffing the visitors' counter alerted me," the doc replied. "She's instructed to sound a warning whenever an outside physician visits. She's too young or otherwise unaware of the literary reference. You couldn't do better than Dr. Zhivago?"

"Someone had entered 'Doctor Moreau,' so that name was taken."

"His name is Max," John said. "Now you know what to expect from him."

"Relative or friend?"

"Friend," John said, rising, struggling to reposition his hospital gown. "Acting as my rearguard."

The doctor didn't know why I laughed. "It's time, John," he

said, which was my cue to leave.

On my subsequent visit, John described what could be seen as the modern man's epic hero's journey—navigating the hospital's sea of expensive diagnostic equipment and medical exams.

I sat opposite him as he reclined on a $10,000 hospital bed. "Record this," he said, opening his laptop. "These are tests I can remember or asked about and chose to note."

After taking a deep breath, he then recited:

"X-ray, MRI, CAT scan, (duplicating exams completed under Dr. Merriwether's care), Ultrasound, Echocardiogram, Magnetoencephalography (twenty-two letters, I counted), Positron Emission Tomography, Fluorescence In Situ Hybridization, Electromyography, Uroscopy, Myelography, Bone Marrow Exam (definitely not fun), Immunologic Blood Test, Enzyme Analysis, Thyroid Function Test. Got all that? Good. I also had my temperature taken with a $350 thermometer. Yes, I asked how much. I have endured more tests than if I had been abducted and probed by aliens. Do you know what they found?"

"Who? The aliens?"

"I'll save you from answering. Nothing." He gave me a look of resignation. Not despair, mind you. He then gazed out the window and shrugged. He was my closest friend, so reading his body language (and there was now a lot of body to read) often substituted for the spoken word.

"So, you've decided to leave?" I asked.

"Near enough," he responded.

After speaking with his family and Jessica, John chose to curtail his involvement with CCH, but only after a consultation with the facility's medical researchers. When asked if they were any closer to a diagnosis, let alone halting the progression of his affliction, they deferred until they obtained feedback from the hospital's newest department, *Artificial Intelligence.*

The AI evaluation process began with computer entry of every medical test, diagnostic procedure, and lab result that John had endured and, going well beyond that, his genetic profile, medical history, family medical history, work history, mental health profile, and dietary habits. Nothing that would appear to be trivial was overlooked, including such nuggets that, at an average rate of 1.254 times a month, he consumed Cheerios floating in two percent milk for breakfast. Terabytes of data were collected, analyzed, and prioritized. Every medical database was cross-referenced and scrutinized, and a disease detection algorithm was applied. Not a scintilla of information was left undigested by the computer. Ones and zeros flowed like blood cells in a throbbing vein.

The effort generated a list of probabilities. Credit the AI Department's lead researcher for being brave enough to share what the computer produced. In retrospect, we learned that Dryden oversold what the AI could reasonably accomplish only to delay John's exit from the hospital.

The researcher cast his eyes about the room, looking for a safe harbor in a sympathetic face. He wisely passed over Amanda, who had grokked that something was seriously wrong, and haltingly addressed John.

"I'd like first to extend an apology. I tried to tamp down expectations. I don't believe that was adequately communicated."

"No need to make excuses," John interrupted. "Best for you to come right out with it."

"The AI generated a list of probabilities," the researcher continued, "the first was acromegaly at .0022 percent. That was, and still is, eliminated as a cause."

A long pause followed, prompting John to say, "And next?"

"And next?" the researcher repeated, looking embarrassed.

"Yes, next," John said. "You mentioned there was a list."

"You might as well tell them," Dryden said.

Glaring at the Administrator, the researcher uttered one word: "Pregnancy."

"Say again?" John asked.

"Pregnancy. A .0003 percent probability."

Considering all the tests he had endured and the lost hope of CCH finding a diagnosis and cure, John could have been angry.

Instead, he laughed. I don't believe I have ever seen him laugh so hard. That is the infectious sentiment that defined my friend at that moment.

In all moments.

Amanda wanted to be angry, but was swayed by her husband's reaction. "I knew it!" she shouted, pointing in my direction. "You two are spending far too much time together!"

"I'm only his friend," I said in mock defense. "A *very close* friend."

Palpably relieved, the researcher tried to explain. "When we queried the AI regarding the result, it referenced John's seven-pound weight gain since admission here at CCH, his increase in ice cream consumption, and the changes to his pelvic and abdominal regions."

"Still, this makes absolutely no sense," Jessica protested. "Why would the AI come up with an impossible result?"

"I asked the same question," the researcher said. "The AI believes that the data entered had errors."

"The AI wasn't quite as fallible as it seems," Jessica offered. "Rather, it believes we are."

Dryden, stoic and silent and offering little, finally chimed in. "You have to understand," he said defensively. "This is not a failure. My hospital has eliminated every known possibility. I can confidently say that John's affliction has never been observed in the annals of human medicine. In the strongest possible terms, I recommend that this hospital be allowed to continue its research."

John looked to Amanda and Jessica for confirmation. Nods were exchanged.

Despite Dryden's protestations, this was my friend's final visit to CCH.

Too BIG: Gary Tarulli

7. OPTIMISTICALLY GOING BROKE

JOHN, IN COMMAND OF his newer, larger rental, a pitch-black SUV he labeled "Death Star," had traversed time and space to arrive at my compact condo.

I live in a gated community. My HOA fee pays for a clubhouse, two noisy pickleball courts, a gym with rows of unused treadmills, and a lap pool. What I do not have is a lawn to mow and virtually no property maintenance responsibilities. For these perks, I relinquish forty percent of my income. Not great, I know, but I could give two shits about building equity in a place to leave the kids I'll never have.

John punched in the secret code necessary to gain admittance through the community's gate. The barrier protects me from Jehovah's Witnesses, but I imagine that the less annoying hordes of the Walking Dead could bust right through.

My friend greeted me as he landed outside my unit and

disembarked. "How does it feel to be a lazy fuck?" was his latest version of impugning my 'lifestyle' or lack thereof.

"It me—lazy and shiftless," I said. "Do me a solid. Save my front door and remember to duck your head coming in."

I hadn't seen my friend in a week, and though I shouldn't have been, I was surprised to see just how big he'd grown. Perhaps there is a psychological component at play when staring up at a person who has breached the seven-foot mark, as he had done, cresting at a magnificent seven feet two inches and weighing a solidly built 261 pounds. An impressive feature of this growth was its exact proportionality. In every conceivable way, the seven-foot-plus John looked precisely like the six-foot-zero John, only bigger. I mean *exactly* the same, from head to big toe. Every hair follicle had grown longer to match his size, and that hair, like mine and yours, grew out and needed cutting. Imagine increasing the display size on your phone or enlarging your computer screen by entering 'Control-Plus' commands. Perfect symmetry. The effect was to render him not only imposing but exceptionally attractive—more so than the 'smaller' John. As I stared, I wondered what an eight-foot friend would look like if the time ever came.

I stood there temporarily transfixed, watching the big man look around in frustration for somewhere appropriate to rest. My condo is sparsely furnished, with nothing befitting his size.

"Try not to break that chair," I finally said.

"When I squeeze my ass into it or hit you with it?"

"I should know better than to make you angry. Try the couch. We can eat lunch at the coffee table. Are you hungry?"

"Does a shark shit in the ocean? Now I'm always hungry."

"Trying to feed you is a tall order," I said, earning a belated groan for the pun.

In advance of my friend's lunchtime visit, I had traveled the usual five suburban miles to the local deli (the kind you see everywhere in the 'burbs), where I had purchased a dozen large rolls, four pounds of sliced roast beef, the equivalent amount Swiss, a few sides packed into those ubiquitous polluting plastic containers, and several bottles of the healthiest juice I could find. John, like me, doesn't drink sugar water, AKA soda. The bill had me wondering if I'd miss the next lease payment on my car.

"I've come to fill you in," John said. "Material for your soon-to-be Pulitzer Prize in literature."

"I've already written my acceptance speech." I retrieved my recorder.

While I ate, John gorged. I listened as my friend brought me up to speed.

"I won't 'bury the lede' as they say in the news business. I am, officially, without a job."

Choking on roast beef, I coughed out: "When did this happen? Did the bastards give you a reason?!"

"Sure did. They told me that I was too big."

"What the hell? How the fuck does that affect *them*?"

"I'm about to explain. The last time I saw you—oh, before I forget, Amanda coerced me into asking if you and Jess did the nasty. She phrased it that delicately. So, now I've asked. You need not answer."

"Tell her it's a work in progress. Like my Pulitzer."

"Better yet, I'll tell her you're 'on the pull.' Remember me mentioning how my coworkers reacted when I was still under seven feet tall? Recently, when they finally started to believe what was happening right before their eyes, they expressed genuine concern. I should clarify. Concern *for* me. They asked questions. I answered. One good question was how I'd get to work and, if I couldn't, what then? I said there'd be plenty of other employment opportunities. Exactly *what* I could be employed as became a game. Window washer, tree trimmer, house painter, and the like were offered as suitable suggestions. I encouraged this nonsense to distract from what might become a real problem."

"Sounds bizarre but innocent enough," I said.

"Trouble was brewing, though. Pass me another roll. The mysteriousness of what was happening to me and my size intimidated my coworkers. Reactions began to change from concern *for* me to concern *about* me. This transition came mostly in the form of polite avoidance. In their eyes, I was becoming more of a character in a grade-B horror movie."

"They went running, hands in the air, screaming?"

"Now *that* would have been comical."

"Something like *Attack of the 50-Foot Woman.*"

"Don't know it."

"A 1950s movie classic. So bad, it's good."

"Curious. What did she wear?"

"I see you've zeroed in on the most important question. Not much. Part of the movie's attraction. But go on. Then what happened?"

"I accidentally overheard one hallway conversation. The topic was whether or not I was contagious."

"What?! Did you respond?"

"No. The recent pandemic has some people thinking that way. Anyway, that's when one of the VPs—I lost track of how many we had at eight—approached me. She said I was no longer a good fit for the corporation. Yes, she actually said 'a good fit,' which made me laugh in her face when I thought about it." John became contemplative and stared off into some imaginary point in space. "Strange how people can get a tad apprehensive when someone like me laughs." Coming back to earth, he looked at me, saying, "And no, I didn't make her run screaming."

"Too bad. Weren't you angry, though? I am."

"The real truth is that I was probably a week, maybe two, away from having a significant problem just getting to work. Even if I could get there, the ergonomics—which were already an issue—would have been untenable. The office chairs were way undersized. I couldn't get my legs under a desk. I was staring down at computer screens."

"Yeah, I can see that happening."

"Other problems occurred in the strangest and most uncomfortable ways."

"You're smiling?"

"In the employee restroom, none of the privacy dividers between urinals were tall enough to stop me from seeing over them. Believe me, I didn't want to. In some countries, men are accustomed to pissing in something resembling a cattle trough. Here, standing next to a coworker at a urinal can get a little awkward, especially when there's no divider. One dude had a sense of humor about it, asking if I was trying to take a gander at his willie."

"Take a gander?" I said. "No one under sixty says that."

"Gander is a name for a male goose. The expression applies to me when you think of a goose stretching its long neck."

"Was that his intention?"

"Don't know. Amusing, though. But not amusing is walking into a stall, and there, squatting one porcelain throne away, is your boss with pants down around his ankles. I did my absolute best not to peer over, but does *he* know that, for fuck's sake?"

Picturing the moment, I started laughing.

John began grinning. "He let one loose just as I made a hasty retreat."

"Jesus," I said, nearly busting a gut. You'd say we were refusing to grow up, though that wasn't exactly true for John.

"Are you going to miss the work?" I asked.

"Not so much, I'll admit. I will miss a few of my colleagues."

John then made a trivial observation that would later prove significant. "Before I left, coworkers threw me an impromptu party. A few voiced regret and insisted on taking selfies with me. 'For remembrance's sake,' they said."

"They'll hire you back when this is over?"

"So they intimated," John answered. "The nature of my job is not conducive to working from home, and company policy wasn't allowing that anyway."

"Amanda is unemployed, and now you are," I said. "I'm sure your medical bills are mounting. With no income, what's next?"

"In the grand scheme of things, what's so important about money? I still have my health." Reflecting on his words, John paused. "That sounded strange, didn't it?"

"A bit."

John flexed a bicep. "I'm healthy as an ox, and big as one, too. Another roll, please. Why do they make them so damn small?"

"You began all this by telling me there had been a couple of setbacks. What's the other one?"

"My health insurance was provided through my employment. No job, no insurance. From now on, I must self-pay for a family health plan under COBRA. Now *that's* a great acronym. Cobra. A snake that bites you in the ass. In this instance, a $25,000 chunk."

"How are you going to manage?"

"For now, by draining my 401(K). I can withdraw without penalty for the medical bills I incur—most of which aren't covered."

"But that's your retirement money ..." I interrupted myself. "Oh, I forgot we're Millennials. We aren't expected to be in the middle class."

John knew I'd offer to help, but he also knew I didn't have a pot to piss in. He leaned back into the sofa to process his food and his thoughts. Grokking my concern for him, he said, "No worries. Given the present circumstances, trying to predict the future is virtually impossible."

I wasn't quite as optimistic. "It would appear to me," I said, "that you just predicted a large chunk of it."

"I did not," my friend insisted. "Most of what I told you has already happened. I don't have to like it, but no one can change it. Predictions mean little. Many never come to pass. Could I or anyone have predicted what's happening to me? Will I become the 50-foot man or as tall as the Eiffel Tower? Or the converse: maybe I'll start getting smaller, disappear into nothingness. None of this means I don't look to the future, like everyone, to plan. But given all the possibilities, don't expect me to worry too much about it."

John's armchair philosophy wasn't all that profound, but it did shed light on how he was able to cope with the giant load of crap life was shoveling his way. And while I did not feel nearly as confident, I felt compelled to be upbeat or try, tamping down my underlying belief that life is a cosmic joke. "Have you seen," I asked, "the '50s movie called *The Incredible Shrinking Man*?"

John smiled. "Shrinking? I am intrigued."

I continued. "Yeah, *shrinking*. Like your finances. This poor sap is on the bow of a little boat when it passes through a mysterious fog bank. Within a few months, he starts shrinking. His clothes hang loose. Bad things happen. Frightened, people shun him. He has money woes. He fights toe-to-paw with the family cat. He battles a spider to the death."

"Out of curiosity," John asked, "how does *his* situation end?"

"That's the part you might find intriguing. Gazing up at the grandness of the night sky, he makes a spiritual connection: The infinitely large to the infinitely small. In doing so, he accepts his fate."

"What you mean to tell me is that the pissant shrank to nothing?"

"In the end, that's the implication."

"It's nice to have a role model in reverse."

"There are some similarities, although I doubt planet Earth can support someone if they become too big."

My friend enveloped a bottle in his hand and drained the last beverage in one fluid motion.

"The part of the story that I like the best," I said, "is that the little fucker ate a whole lot less than you."

Preparing to leave, John unfolded himself from my sofa. "I'll be returning for dinner. I like my cow medium rare."

"Before you go," I said, "I have a job for you."

"What's that?"

My living room has a ten-foot ceiling. I pointed up to the overhead light fixture. "That bulb needs changing."

8. KARDASHIAN'S ASS

SOON AFTER JOHN'S LAST visit to CCH, he became a public figure. As per Merriam-Webster, that means "an individual or entity that has acquired fame or notoriety or has participated in a particular public controversy." He did not choose or want to be defined as such. If it takes a particular personality type to crave public attention, my friend certainly didn't have it.

"Better stock up on TP," I heard him say to Amanda. "I believe living our lives will soon become a shit show."

The remark was spot on. When John emerged from his home (now less frequently due to the unwanted attention), one or more reporters and photographers were waiting. Disguising himself was impossible. Wearing a fake nose, mustache, and glasses would have— merely and conspicuously—rendered him a 275-pound, seven-foot-four-inch man sporting a phony nose, mustache, and glasses.

What started the attention is uncertain, but photos of John taken during his last day at work by a former fellow employee began appearing on Facebook. They soon gravitated to other social media platforms such as X, YouTube, WeChat, Instagram, WhatsApp, LinkedIn, and others. Much of the content was inaccurate and insulting. Posting online brings out the worst devils in human nature.

Taking the attacks in stride, John showed me one thread that I regurgitated in part below with spelling and grammar errors intact. My comments are in italics. The thread begins with a ridiculous post and spirals rapidly downhill from there.

jcmash: Where does this John fellow come from if that's his real name? Why is it being kept secret?

tcz: It's not a secret. His identity is public record.

jcmash: You're dilusionel if you don't believe the government is involved.

tcz: How does that make any sense? What would that accomplish?

jcmash: Try not to be a f*cking moron. *(Asterisk to avoid censorship. You can insult, but don't curse while doing so.)*

tcz: You are as retarded as your spelling. *(Posters quickly succumb to the lowest common denominator.)*

fedup: The man's an illegal alien. *(Troll joins the party.)*

jcmash: I knew it.

blvanon: No doubt he's an alien, but what kind?

x-factor: The man gotta be part Watusi. They're tall.

jcmash: Like Obama. He's Watusi.

The 'chat' degrades until posters appear to be auditioning as comedy writers for late-night TV. In a fit of masochism, I began counting the entries on this thread, self-preservation stopping me at 136. When I referred to the posters as idiots, John was more charitable. "Makes you wonder, doesn't it?" he remarked. "Are people so lonely that they feel compelled to devote their time to such nonsense?"

In deference to my friend's tolerant perspective, I said: "We've come a long way from the art of letter writing between acquaintances.

Now, civil discourse is mostly strangers chatting through social media. Only it's not so civil anymore, is it?"

"Certainly does appear that way," John said, adding: "I've heard it labeled 'anti-social' media."

"We Millennials are addicted to the internet," I said, "but more so are the Gen Z'ers. TikTok, YouTube, and Instagram are akin to catnip until the next best thing comes along. Being a bystander to the craziness can be amusing. Do you recall when, several years ago, a photo of Kim Kardashian's sumptuous naked ass went viral? There was serious talk that downloads of the image would break the internet. It didn't quite happen, but for a short time, her shiny booty was the subject of nearly one percent of all web browsing in the U.S."

"A lot of men wanted to put frosting on that cake," John said, smiling, attempting to imitate the curved shape of an ass with his large, outstretched hands.

"Helen of Troy was 'the face that launched a thousand ships.' Kardashian's ass launched a million tweets." I stared at John. "You know, this conversation has me thinking. Are you up for an internet challenge? Can you imagine the attention you'd get from a picture of *your* naked backside?"

"File that under 'Max's *Asinine* Ideas.'" John said, emphasizing the word. "You have a file cabinet full of them."

"On a more serious note, what do your kids think of the attention you're receiving?"

"Why not ask them yourself?"

John yelled up the stairs. "Carrie! Brad! We have a guest! Get your fannies down here!"

"I didn't mean for you to bother them."

"Nonsense. Maybe they'll be more open with you than with me."

Entering the room together, the siblings greeted me with an effusive "Hi, Maxie," followed by Carrie demanding, "Where's Jess? Isn't she coming?"

"Sorry, not today, sweetheart," I said, then watched her face contort to a scowl of disappointment, the special look young girls are adept at making.

"Max wants to ask you both something," John said.

I wasn't sure how to phrase the question. I stumbled out, "Your dad's on the internet. What do you think about that?"

"My friends and I aren't on those sus sites so much," Brad said. "I'm mostly playing soccer or video games. Dad tells me to ignore that trash stuff."

Carrie, younger and more impressionable, left me with a different feeling. Her face turned gloomy as she curtly said: "They're all cursed." She then quickly spun herself around and vanished back upstairs.

After I debated with Brad as to whether Pelé or Messi was the all-time best football player, he, too, disappeared.

John said this about his daughter: "I'll talk with her later. Amanda and I are trying our best, but it's a fine line between protecting and overprotecting. For better or worse, social websites are a large part of their world. Sooner or later, they'll have to learn how to cope with them."

Inevitably, it was through the internet that John's story became widely and quickly disseminated. It soon merited the attention of over-the-air and print media and their web-based affiliates and outlets. To this point, no one had gained access to John or his medical records. The only information available was photographs of a six-foot John and contemporary ones identifying him as the same person, only significantly taller and broader. Essentially, they lacked what a good journalist calls "facts."

This absence in no way hindered speculation. As John continued to grow bigger, so too did the distortions concerning him. The media circus was back in town, with each outlet authoring a version of the story to serve a specific target audience. What follows are excerpts from podcasts, newspaper editorials, and magazine articles:

Sports In View: It would be fair to require that this person be prohibited from engaging in almost every area of sports competition. There is a particular urgency if he should continue to grow. What personal record in basketball, football, and weightlifting, to name a few, would not be shattered by him? A professional team that placed this person under contract would have an insurmountable competitive advantage. Are we to witness asterisks in every record book?

Get Healthy/Stay Healthy!: After consulting experts in a wide range of disciplines, the likelihood of steroid abuse presents itself. Although not yet conclusively proven, nothing else can adequately explain this individual's dramatic increase in muscle mass.

Freakish: What was predicted in these pages long ago now appears to have finally happened! By design or some experiment gone awry, we may be witnessing a genetically engineered superhuman who excels in size and strength, and who knows what else. There will be no limits. It takes little imagination to forecast humans dwarfing even the largest of Earth's creatures.

The Scientific Method: The media is full of ill-considered speculation concerning this person, much of it centered on the potential trajectory of his growth. While it is safe to conclude (judging from the available evidence, scant as it may be) that John appears to be steadily increasing both in height and body mass, it is *inaccurate* to propose that this growth has no upper limit. For mammals, consideration must be given to Galileo's Square-Cube Law, the neurophysiology of pumping blood, and maintaining proper body temperature.

Guffaw: Our faithful online readers have responded by submitting suggestions concerning both the pitfalls and the advantages of living a life while being monstrous in size. Here are a few of our favorites, chosen from hundreds of submissions:

He could:

Put a leash on a giraffe and walk it as a pet.

Earn 'big bucks' filling hot air balloons ... with his breath.

Drain swimming pools instantly by doing a cannonball.

Enter and win every hot dog eating contest.

With-It Women: (Cover Stories) Inside! Eight Secrets on How to Enjoy Sex When Your Man Is *Exceedingly* Well-Endowed. This Time Size *Does* Matter.

Man UP! (Two articles)

Will We See a New World Record for Penis Size?

Find Out If Your Junk Measures Up—A Statistical Comparison.

Modern Style: Will Big and Tall Be the Latest Rage?

Nutrition and Diet: Diet and Height: Foods That Can Make You Grow.

Verdant Earth: There is an issue begging for our attention, unintentionally exemplified by this solitary person, and that is the dire impact every one of us has on an environment that can no longer sustain our abuse. As John continues to grow, so do we all in terms of population and individual consumption.

When the allegations, theories, and conspiracy theories became abusive, John called the Squad together to solicit advice. We were four, but a fifth was involved, an excellent bottle of Japanese whiskey our host had been saving. Gratifying to me was how my friends had begun to treat Jessica like fam.

A lively exchange of ideas ensued. We considered the media our adversary, seeking some way to counterattack. An hour went by. We were partway into the discussion—and the bottle—with nothing meaningful to show.

"Reminds me of an expression," John mused. "In war, truth is the first casualty."

"It *is* war, and the enemy needs to be on the wrong side of a firing squad." It was Amanda who voiced this. Figuratively speaking, I want to believe.

"It's not as if people in the media know me," John countered, doing his 'glass-half-full' thing. "Deep down, it's hard to be too angry."

"Yeah," she responded, "but on the surface, it's *real* easy."

"Max and I aren't leaving here without giving you both some options," Jessica insisted. "We're in this together."

I agreed. "Between us, we're bound to come up with something. One thing is for sure: you're too big to go into hiding."

Amanda shook her head at my stupidity, but she was smiling. "You really said that, didn't you?"

We wasted a second hour proposing bad ideas. During an interlude, Jessica commented on the silky softness of the whiskey, which led to a contest of sorts on just how fabulously smooth it was— ice, glass, bowling balls, a baby's behind, six-hundred-thread-count sheets. I had trouble explaining to the ladies, "Kim Kardashian's polished ass." John won with "The Mirror on the James Webb Space Telescope," while Jessica's "The surface of the monolith in *2001: A Space Odyssey* was disqualified as a fictional object.

As to the matter at hand, we seemed to be at an impasse when, partly out of frustration, Jessica blurted out, "They say 'if you can't beat them, join them.'"

I watched her face take on that look you get when you slowly realize that you might be on to something.

The idea was all Jessica's; it just needed a little coaxing. "There's another apt expression," I said: "'There's no such thing as bad publicity.'"

"You'd be a natural!" Amanda exclaimed, catching on and mulling the possibilities over in her mind. "Big and handsome ..."

"Oh, no," John interrupted. "Not so fast! Where *I* go, sweetheart, *you* go."

I was enjoying Amanda's discomfort when John pointed one long finger at me and said, "And *you*. Do you remember our deal? This could be the perfect opportunity to cash in on free publicity."

"Hey, you can always count me in," I said.

The three of us shifted our attention to Jessica. Without hesitation, she said: "Same. What would it say about me if you did this without your personal physician?"

We spent the remainder of the evening strategizing the where and how of public appearances.

As Jess and I were leaving, I approached Amanda. "What gives? You didn't once ask, 'Are you two doing it?'"

"No, but she did ask me," Jessica volunteered, smiling.

"What did you tell her?"

"Yaas."

9. TOO SMALL

HOPING TO BRING A level of sanity to the public discourse concerning his affliction, John authorized a limited release of his medical records. The action had the opposite effect of what was intended, for it merely fanned the flames of public speculation. As in most things, he took the setback in stride.

Public opinion split into distinct groups. Some believed that medical science would ultimately provide a reasonable (and therefore comforting) explanation for my friend's disorder. In contrast, others attributed it to some unknown and nefarious plan of action—the scheming of a government or corporate entity, or even a rogue billionaire. The Illuminati were given a pass.

A small fringe group was disinclined to accept the existence of John entirely. The media, they said, was responsible for the hoax, fabricating a human-interest story to bolster ratings. This argument might have swayed me if I had not witnessed what was happening to John with my own eyes.

One sentiment unified all but the skeptics: Fascination with the nature and trajectory of John's inexplicable growth. The public began clamoring for him to step into the spotlight, appear in the flesh (quite substantially), and subject himself to a live interview. The Squad had no issue with close engagement, even knowing that interviews frequently devolve into interrogations. "Let the battle be joined," Amanda liked to say.

Because there is strength in numbers, John told the media we were a package deal. Take it or leave it. Although we could cherry-pick where we would appear (there now appeared to be only Liberal or Conservative venues), John couldn't care less. In his estimation and mine, the 'news' was pandering to what the audience wanted to hear and believe. No matter how grim the story, it was all about entertainment for the masses.

And we did entertain. In a live interview, little is scripted except, on occasion, the interviewer's questions. John told us that he respected our judgment and would enjoy whatever we wanted to say. "Why hold back?" he said. "That's what most people do. The truth shall set ye free."

Maybe so, I thought, but sometimes that freedom seems a long time coming.

Days before our first live television appearance, my friend's newfound notoriety reaped a benefit.

Having recently signed a lucrative multi-year contract with an Italian sports franchise, the starting center of an NBA basketball team was temporarily vacating his opulent estate. The player, Karter, aware of John's increasingly untenable living conditions (he, too, once lived in a home that had become too small and too visible to the public eye), offered up his 'crib' for John and his family to reside in. "Hey, no worries, man," he said. "I need a caretaker, so you'd be doing me a solid watching the place till I get back. If you need better-fitting duds, I'll get you the name of my tailor."

The residence, custom-built for a taller man, presented the Whitmores with the perfect alternative to their besieged home. For starters, it was protected by a monitored security gate, behind which were five acres of neatly manicured lawn, a custom pool, and a regulation basketball court..

The living area, with ten-foot ceilings and oversized furnishings, was too big for most, but this presented less concern than if they had been too small. Two of the residence's bedroom suites were designed to accommodate visiting family members and Karter's vertically challenged, sub-six-foot friends. These rooms were perfect for Brad and Carrie. Both were delighted with the novelty of the mansion, Brad especially, having named it "The Magic Johnson Kingdom," though it had nothing to do with that player.

The bedroom suite, now occupied by John and Amanda, had a walk-in closet larger than many NYC apartments. The closet had been emptied except for a solitary box on top of which was a scribbled note: "Yours. Taking up too much room." (Karter, it seems, had a sense of humor.) Inside the box was a new pair of Komfort footwear, a popular brand endorsed by the player and easily identified by the big stylized "*K*" logo on the side of each shoe. A note fell out: "Sorry if too small."

Left behind as an afterthought by Karter, the footwear would unexpectedly take on a significance far beyond its intrinsic value.

Knowing that his family was adequately settled in their new abode, John mustered us for what was to be our most memorable live television appearance, one that cemented the public's view of him. The network in question was popular despite being unfair and unbalanced. One host, now gone, had sold his soul to acquire the silver tongue of the devil. (Although his tongue had been tarnished, his words still shone like a beacon of truth to his ever-faithful flock.) His replacement, Ed Narre, had proven himself to be a lesser clone, but we still had our work cut out for us, for there was a shit-ton of misinformation to rectify during our appearance.

Karter had granted permission to use his home, and the first interview was staged in the mansion's sunroom. The broadcast went live after light and sound checks were made by the camera crew. The session started innocently enough, with the host (who had chosen to remain in the studio) identifying us and then summarizing what the public knew or thought they knew about John.

Jessica sat next to me on one of the four studio-provided chairs. She directed my attention to a monitor where we could observe what the cameras captured for the at-home audience. Instead of the typical image restricted to the guests' faces and shoulders, the cameras frequently panned out to view John in his entirety, effectively calling attention to his relative size.

Believing I had nothing tangible to offer, Narre tried to dispense with me first. "My producer," he began, "has described you as, what *exactly* was that again? Merely a friend?" The intent, communicated by a sarcastic tone and pinched eyebrows, was to marginalize anything I managed to say during the interview.

Being the target of the first shot fired, I took issue. "Listen," I said, emphasizing the word. "As a *close* friend of John, I have been with him from the start. Who would be better at offering first-hand insight if the opportunity arises?"

Disappointingly, my remark failed to elicit a response, only a quick redirect to Jessica, who was next in line for some superficial soundbite scrutiny.

"As John Whitmore's doctor," Narre began, "you claim to be qualified to answer questions concerning his present condition. Interestingly, you appear unable, some might say ill-prepared, to do so."

I didn't have long to wonder how Jessica would respond to the implied insult. "I can satisfy your apparent concern about my credentials," she said. "Your audience should know that as a doctor of endocrinology, I completed four years of college, four years in medical school ...

"...*Harvard* graduate," Amanda interrupted. "*Second* in her class."

"...three years of residency, two more in fellowship, and I am Board certified by the American Board of Internal Medicine ...

"Yes, but ..." Narre tried to interrupt

"...I have authored and co-authored several published articles, and have been nominated twice for a Laureate Award. OK, I'll stop there. You get the picture. And yes, numerous experts in the medical and scientific disciplines and I have failed to determine the cause of John's affliction. We did, however, rule out what it *isn't*. Unfortunately, there still is a lot of misinformation on the internet and elsewhere."

"That's what we are here to clarify," Narre claimed, then tried to lay the groundwork for doing the opposite. "The facts, even when unpleasant, do seem to have a way of coming out, despite efforts to suppress them."

I had expected the host to capitalize on the widely held suspicions swirling around John. He was throwing enough shade to darken the planet. I turned to John, who had yet to be asked a question, and said, "May I?"

"Be my guest," he said. "You're the wordsmith."

"You're correct about one thing, Ed," I said. "Facts have been ignored. Buried under all the bullshit being reported by your outlet." So much for 'wordsmith,' I thought.

"We'll set that comment aside ... for now," Narre deflected. He turned to John. "Thank you, Mr. Whitmore, for allowing our cameras into your home. But it's not your home, is it?"

"No," John replied. "I would rather like to think of it as a temporary sanctuary."

"Sanctuary?" Narre said with a scornful laugh. "That's hard to believe. For a person your size? Sanctuary from whom or God knows what is the question."

"I expressed the understandable desire for privacy for myself and my family. I never suggested being afraid."

"Ah. Fear. That may be the right word. Shouldn't people be

afraid of *you,* as many people are? I mean, why wouldn't they be? After all, just to be near you can be a little intimidating."

Amanda headed off John's reply. "Oh, he didn't mean to frighten you!" she said. Staring at Narre, she contorted her face into a mock look of dread. "Good thing you're safely there in your studio."

A muffled laugh escaped from one of the camera operators. Because the broadcast was live, the sound made it on air. Later, when I studied a rebroadcast of the interview, I noticed that the laugh had been conveniently edited out.

"Be careful what you say," John volunteered, smiling at Narre. "If you knew my wife, you'd be more frightened of *her.*"

Narre, seemingly unfazed, took the opportunity to zero in on Amanda.

That was a mistake.

"I can only imagine," he began, "how—and I'll attempt to be discreet here—*intimacy* has changed between you and your husband."

"You imagine? Is that a fact?" Amanda said. "I can tell you that *intimacy* between John and me will never change. Let me guess, though, you're really talking about sex, aren't you, you bad, bad boy? Well, keep imagining if that's what gets you off." Pausing briefly, she added: "You know, it's a good thing that John and I live in a gated home."

"And why is that?" ventured our host.

"The extra security prevents people like you from peering in our bedroom window late at night."

Amanda's clapback produced a delighted "High-key, girl!" from Jessica. Ignoring Narre and the forty million people watching, she 'high-fived' Amanda in celebration. I watched the poor cameraman insert a chunk of his fist in his mouth, then bite down hard to stop himself from laughing.

John and I, however, were under no compunction. We had no sympathy for the host. "Take my advice," I cautioned him. "Stay down for the count."

And, in a manner, that's what he did, by breaking for a

commercial. I took the opportunity to lean over and whisper in Amanda's ear. "Hypocrite. Like you never asked me about *my* sex life."

When the break was over, Narre took a different tack. "You've pretty much been a mystery, John," he said. "Let's find out what people really want to learn about you. Care to take a call or two?"

"Of course."

"Good. Bill, you're on the air."

"Thanks for taking my call. My six-year-old son has a question."

"What's his name?" John asked.

"Oliver. He's listening."

"I'd like to speak to Oliver if he doesn't mind. Hi, Oliver. You have a question for me?"

"Uh-huh," came a timid voice. "Do you have superpowers?"

"No ... but your mom just might."

"Really? Nah ..."

"Does she sometimes know what you're thinking?"

"I guess."

"Well, that's a superpower. Most moms have it."

"Really!? That's dope!"

The next caller asked what political party John was registered with.

"Mostly, I vote for the Democrat, but it's hard to pull the lever sometimes when the candidate's integrity is suspect."

"You're a Democrat appearing on a Conservative show?" the caller questioned. "You believe in keeping your friends close and your enemies closer?"

"*If* I were to call them an enemy, why not? How can you make an enemy your friend if they're not close?"

And so it went—we deflected, absorbed, and countered statements ranging from profane to inane. All was going as well as expected. When not responding to questions, John sat there bemused, pleased with how his Squad was doing. The mood rapidly changed, however, when Narre gambled at recapturing the initiative by deliberately and transparently attempting to piss my friend off.

"Without an explanation," Narre sermonized, "as to what is happening to you—I mean a plausible explanation that we can all believe—should you be considered an aberration? A freak of nature? As a parent, what do your children think? Are they embarrassed?"

Rarely have I seen John angry, and only when his family and friends were the subjects of attack. But what passes for anger in most people is not the same for my friend. For him, Narre's provocative remarks represented an opportunity. Slowly, leveling his gaze at the man, John rose. I caught his remarkable image on the TV monitor, which captured all seven feet and six inches of him. Impressive. Because he was so damn big and so good-looking, and I'm something of a Trekkie, the sight of him reminded me of the statuesque Greek god Apollo in an old *Star Trek* episode.

"You know, Narre," he began, "I have avoided being confrontational because plenty of things in this life are more important than your trivialities. But it's tough to remain polite when you have subjected my wife and friends to your mocking sneers and trash statements, spoken under the guise of being informed about us when, quite obviously, you are not. Now, you bring the most precious thing I have—my kids—into this mess you created. You see, Narre, some may think that I am too big physically. I can cope with that. But I wonder how you cope—considering how you act and think—with being too small?"

With that, John turned. Surprising everyone, he looked straight into the television camera and said: "Your audience deserves better. We're done here. Out you go."

He never raised his voice. Amanda and Jessica followed him to another part of the house while I stayed behind to ensure the crew packed up and left without incident. I had fun with the two cameramen, joking about the many ways we could call Narre a prick.

The interview and the few that followed failed to stop the inaccurate stories about John. We weren't going to change the fundamentals of human nature, which also dictate that the public's fascination with him would eventually fade over time.

There was, however, a notable shift in the type of attention my friend was now receiving. The adept way he (and, to a lesser degree, Amanda, Jessica, and I) navigated the media appearances resulted in John being universally known and immensely popular. People have a great affinity for someone willing to be self-effacing while speaking unadulterated truth, simply because those desirable qualities seem so hard to find.

While I, for the most part, was ignored, the public's interest was temporarily diverted to Amanda and Jessica. Riding on John's considerable coattails, they received fifteen minutes of fame. The women in the audience had John to swoon over. Now the men had my two attractive lady friends to ogle. One tabloid headline, a bit of an ego crusher for me, read: "Giant John's Surgeon Dating Little-Known Writer." The piece was accompanied by a photograph of Jessica in a bikini, gleaned from the internet, where nothing goes to die.

As for Amanda, a women's magazine complimented her talent of not taking bullshit from a man, unoriginally referring to her as "The Mouth That Roared."

Both women declined six-figure offers to pose nude on a popular men's website.

Too BIG: Gary Tarulli

10. "BIG" BUSINESS

JOHN BECAME THE RECIPIENT of another stroke of good luck, and the way this came about requires a brief explanation.

During the live-on-the-air interview with Narre, the camera crew decided that one way to accentuate John's size was to focus on his huge footwear, the new pair of *Kicks* given to him by Karter, basketball's star center. John had worn the shoes solely because they were the only ones that comfortably fit him.

The five-second image of a pair of shoes would never have become a big deal, except that corporations have done their utmost to make us into their living, breathing billboards. (Try to purchase an item of sporting apparel without a company name or identifiable logo prominently plastered somewhere on it.) The pair of *Kicks,* better known as Karter Kicks, was seen by millions of viewers and was readily recognizable in that precise way. If life can change on a dime, why not the letter K?

Initially, none of this registered with the four of us. But it was very much noticed by the company that manufactured the shoes, specifically the creative folks in the advertising division, who would have been remiss to pass up the opportunity for publicity. They saw a huge one here, served on a silver platter by a strikingly handsome, physically fit, and hugely popular man who just might be convinced to be the symbol for their corporate brand.

The advertising department's idea gained momentum when the company's accounting department reported a twelve percent uptick in *Kicks'* online retail sales in the two days immediately following John's television appearance. Moreover, sporadic reports from brick-and-mortar stores indicated that *Ks* were beginning to 'fly off the shelves.' Within a few days, every store was out of stock. The news ascended the corporate ladder, rapidly reaching the top rung. The enthused CEO perched there decided to contact my friend.

The Whitmore finances are crucial to understanding how John reacted. They were beyond broke. The family insurance policy did not cover the six-figure-and-growing medical expenses, and John and Amanda were unemployed. The use of John's IRA for medical costs had initially helped, but like their drained bank accounts, that source was depleted. Losing their home had become a real possibility. Filing for Chapter 7 bankruptcy would ruin their credit rating for several years. In sum, there would have to be draconian and unpleasant changes to their lifestyle. Beyond the unpaid bills, which hung like the Sword of Damocles over his head, there was one more thing for my friend to consider: How long could his body sustain his present growth rate?

With all this occupying his mind, John, who never considered himself well-suited to selling the public anything, did something out of character. After learning what might be proposed in general terms, he agreed to meet company reps at Komfort's headquarters in Atlanta. A corporate jet was provided for him, Amanda, and whoever else he chose to bring along. Jessica, who was in the enviable position to observe the world's most unique medical case, had been granted unlimited leave from the corporate practice.

As for myself, well, I had no work schedule to adjust.

A debit card with a $10,000 balance was provided to John for 'expenses.' The corporate representative explained: "It was money already earned many times over for the nice little bump in Komfort footwear sales." The unexpected 'generosity' gave us ample reason to prepare for the meeting. We implemented an internet search to find the intrinsic advertising value of John being John. Our efforts led to several contracts that the famous had signed endorsing a product or service. Sometimes, the endorsement entailed the use of their recognizable image.

We had an idea of what we would find, yet the dollar amounts were staggering to contemplate—contracts in the tens of millions. A few deals were reported to be over one hundred million dollars, with wealthy celebrities becoming much more prosperous. Many, such as Karter, were athletes.

We wondered aloud what amount John could command if he were willing.

"I'm shocked!" Amanda shouted, pointing out a dollar amount that caused my brain to seize. "Who would have believed a boxer would earn that much money from selling a grill? A famous chef—that I could believe. But a *boxer?!*"

"What bothers me the most," Jessica said, "and I'm speaking as a doctor, are the athletes who endorse soda. They project a healthy image, then use it to sell a drink that is the antithesis of the healthful diet necessary to attain it."

"The unbridled joys of capitalism," I responded. "Did you find out what kind of deal Karter got?"

"Twenty-seven million, and I'm not cappin'," John said. "He's the first I checked."

I whistled my appreciation. "Care to venture a guess how you would compare? Keep in mind that you're my B-F-F."

"You're an A-S-S," John responded, stretching his long legs. "And the answer is no, not exactly."

We opened Komfort Footwear's website and were not always happy with the ads we saw.

"I remember," Jessica commented, "my father once said there was a time when sneakers were inexpensive. Back when wearing *Keds* wasn't a fashion statement."

"Anything can be hyped," I said.

A flight attendant returned to ask if we wanted more canapés or refills of the bubbly. Amanda, never one to hold back, suggested she leave the bottle.

"John, are you sure you don't want an attorney or agent?" Jessica asked, refilling our crystals with Cristal.

It was not the first time one of us had broached the subject of legal representation. From the start, John's response had been vague but consistent: "That might come later. I've decided to proceed a bit differently." He did not share what that meant, though Amanda appeared to know. My impression was that he was holding something back. Hours later, I understood why.

We began our descent into Atlanta. As ground features resolved into focus, the perception of our altitude increased. John, staring out one of the cabin's overlarge windows, made a derisive comment:

"Look at those puny people down there. They're like pathetic little ants."

Turning, he saw three shocked faces. Grinning, he had another comment:

"Gotcha."

A limo greeted us at the airport and took us to the Four Seasons Hotel. Jessica and I were put in the same room, making us wonder how the hospitality staff at Komfort knew of our relationship. We weren't complaining, and Amanda was delighted. Our accommodations were prepaid, and meals were charged to the debit card provided. In yet another fortunate turn of events, John used the same card to pay a small portion of his outstanding debts. Small—like in those bills for essential electric, gas, and water services.

The following day, the same limo transported us to Komfort headquarters, where we were greeted by a fawning team of suits who escorted us via a glass-walled elevator to the fortieth-floor office. The panoramic city view was stunning, a vast expanse of downtown Atlanta glimmering in the orange light of a midmorning sun.

A massive slab of rosewood weighed down the center of the room. Gazing at the table, Amanda introduced herself with a comment: "Now we know where the Amazon Rainforest went."

A smiling woman extended a hand. "You must be Amanda Whitmore. None of you needs introductions, but I imagine we do. I'm Grace Conway, CEO. Grace, if you please."

Conway, perhaps in her late forties, wore the obligatory woman's blazer and a V-neck blouse. In today's woke world, I wondered if the plunge of the "V" had to be measured to the millimeter to ensure it was appropriate for the office environment. She appeared to have measured correctly, hitting the right note of professional confidence without losing her femininity. She made another introduction: "This is my Head of Advertising, Barry Krasner."

In his thirties, Krasner wore a dark suit set off by a tie so colorful and bright you'd need to avert your eyes for risk of blindness. His sharp facial features and narrow-set eyes made me wonder if he was there to be Conway's attack dog. He looked the part.

There was a bit of a shuffle as people sought their places around the table. The commotion provided Jessica enough time to lean into John and, concerning Conway, say, "Careful with that one. She's a wolf in sheep's clothing." Good advice, I thought. You don't rise to the apex of a billion-dollar corporation without being clever and aggressive.

A VP of Marketing, an attorney, and a number cruncher were, in turn, introduced. They were relegated to answering questions directed to them by the CEO. The overall impression was that Conway did not want to overwhelm us with too much corporate jargon.

The Squad occupied chairs on one side of the table. John's considerable bulk did not present a problem, the company having previously wooed Karter and other tall athletes.

Conway began the show.

"I have to say, Mr. Whitmore... "

"...John, if you please."

"John. It was certainly my company's good fortune, and now maybe yours, that the public saw you wearing our footwear."

"You realize that my wearing Komforts was happenstance. They were very recently given to me by Karter."

"Yes, we thought that a strong possibility, knowing you reside in his home. But, going beyond that, you came across exceptionally well on live TV. Especially gratifying was how you handled yourself, I'll come right out and say it—with that *asshole*, Narre. Priceless."

"'Priceless?'" Amanda repeated. "We're counting on that."

"Well, that's what we're here to discuss," Conway said, chuckling. "Is calling you Amanda OK?"

"I can't see why not," Amanda said guardedly. "For the time being, anyway."

"No worries. I'm sure we'll reach an agreement. As you may know, forty million people watched that broadcast."

"Yes," I chimed in. "And once word got out just how entertaining that broadcast was, another thirty million watched when it went viral on YouTube." Then, to emphasize my point, I held up my hand, making a *"K"* by spreading my index and forefinger wide, then placing my thumb to bisect the two. "The audience demographic was favorable, too: twenty-four- to thirty-nine-year-olds. They purchase forty percent of your shoes."

"I see you've done your homework, Max," Conway said. She didn't seem particularly appreciative that I had done so. "Will you be acting as John's agent?"

I was there to assist my friend in any way I could.

"I'm his wingman," I simply said.

"He's also my agent," John added.

"I am?"

"You are now. Agents get ten percent of whatever contract is negotiated."

That *was* a surprise. I didn't ask why I deserved even one dollar, so I quipped: "That's big of you."

Krasner decided to speak. He shouldn't have.

"I'll give you credit," he said, addressing John. "That whole thing you did with that kid, the one thinking you might have superpowers, was pure show."

"Only it wasn't 'show.'"

"Whatever it was, it was convincing."

"I told you what it was."

Conway gave Krasner a 'shut-the-fuck-up' stare. "What Barry means to say," she attempted to clarify, "is that you come across as genuine. From our point of view, that is a great attribute."

"Can we build on that thought?" John said. "I'd like to discuss ad content. If I'm to appear in any ads, they must reflect what the public should hear, but they seldom do."

"And what would that be?"

"The truth."

A mix of expressions came from the corporate side of the table: annoyance, confusion, anger. I had hoped the meeting would turn fun, even though I'd be lying if I said the prospect of losing ten percent of millions wasn't in the back of my mind.

"I beg your pardon?" Conway said, responding to John. "Are you implying we're deliberately lying?"

"Not at all. Lying is easily detectable. 'Misleading' is the kinder word."

"And how do we do that?" an irritated Krasner asked, his face rivaling his tie in color.

"Through distortion, exaggeration, or omission. Regrettably, your ad policy reflects what is all too common in the industry. I'm only singling out your company because, if I allow it, my face would appear in your ads."

"Care to give us an example?" Conway asked.

"Many of your footwear ads overstate performance and health claims."

"Be more specific," Krasner insisted.

"One of the sneaker lines you sell implies wearing them will make you jump higher."

"And your walkers aren't the cure for plantar fasciitis," Jessica said. "On the flight here, I saw an ad like that on your website."

"There's something Max shared with me," John said. "The 'vegan' line of footwear you manufacture is made from petroleum products."

"So what?" Krasner said. "You're criticizing us for trying to reduce our carbon footprint?"

"Vegan shoes are made using toxic chemicals," I responded. "They also contain plastics or synthetic fibers that enter the ecosystem, and most do not biodegrade easily. 'Vegan' may help save an animal, but stop pretending you are saving the planet."

Sidestepping, Conway addressed John, asking, "Are they comfortable?" Judging from the sarcasm in her voice, I think we were beginning to piss her off.

"Very," John responded. "Or I wouldn't be here."

The other side of the table was still listening. That told me a lot. Conway turned to Amanda and asked:

"I suppose you, too, have a complaint?"

"Now that you ask," she said. "Yes, I do, as a parent. One style of your sneakers retails for more than two hundred dollars. Stop targeting young inner-city kids who quickly grow out of them. Parents feel compelled to buy another pair, spending money they might not have had in the first place."

At this point, Conway was probably wondering why we

seemed intent on self-destruction. Our negotiating skills did seem to be sorely lacking.

"Impractical," she remarked. "If we implement half of your suggestions, our profits will take a nosedive."

"Would they?" I asked. "You know damn well that the young people who recently bought the *K*s were attracted to the honesty they saw in John. Why not give them more of it? Do you believe they want to be fed the same tired old BS?"

I stared at Conway. She stared back. I don't think she liked me, and my speech had no discernible positive effect on her. Amanda decided to give negotiating a try. "Haven't you seen *Miracle on 34th Street*?" she asked the CEO. "It's one of those uplifting Christmas movies."

There were a few tentative nods and a smile or two, so she continued: "When it helped Macy's shoppers, Kris Kringle, acting as the store's Santa, recommends a competitor. Gimbels, I believe. Anyway, Macy's customers loved the honesty. Ultimately, the goodwill policy helped the store's bottom line."

"Lovely," Conway clapped back. "Just lovely. So now you want us to play Santa Claus? Sounds delightful. We can't afford the luxury." She paused a second before uttering: "And, by the way, neither can you."

There it was! I knew the veiled reference to John's fiscal woes might come into play. Conway and company did their homework. I had also done mine, and this wasn't over. John probably knew most of what I was about to say, but personality-wise, I was far better suited to play the part of 'bad cop.' Besides, I was now his agent. I had to earn my keep—time to go savage.

"Actually, it's your corporation that can't afford to pass up a deal," I said.

"Oh, yeah, and how do you figure that?" Krasner asked with a sneer. He didn't like me either.

"Your last quarterly earnings report showed a nine percent

decline in year-over-year sales and a twelve percent hit in net operating income. The price per share of your common stock has declined twenty percent from one year ago. Komfort's share of the footwear market has been steadily eroding."

I paused there, even though I had one more card to play: There were rumors of Conway being ousted as CEO. If the board cleaned house, Krasner was likely to go with her. Judging by what she said next, she guessed I knew all this.

"John," Conway said, deliberately ignoring me. "I have to wonder. If you hadn't brought up your concerns, and we'll try to address them, you might have negotiated a more lucrative contract. So why do it?"

"The public learns about these endorsement deals and thinks them obscene. So do I."

"That's how business is usually done."

"Doesn't make it right. Ultimately, the cost of the endorsements is passed along to the consumer."

"You aren't going to change that, you know," Conway stated.

"True. I can only apply the idea to myself."

"There is still an outstanding issue, John—your health. I have no way of expressing this without being blunt. Will you be able to execute the terms of a contract?"

"I can give you that assurance," Jessica volunteered. "As his physician."

"John?" Conway asked. "Will you be employing Dr. Merriwether as your hired personal physician?"

"He will," Amanda asserted.

Now Jessica was surprised. "You will?" she asked both.

"How does five percent sound?" John suggested, an enticement he did not have to make. Later, he would pay all the overdue medical bills incurred at her office.

Detailed contract discussions ensued. Lunch came catered in. Hours later, many of the contract provisions had been worked out.

John's image would appear in a limited number of TV, print, and internet ads. The company stipulated specific modifications to its advertising policy. The pro-people advertising changes would themselves be touted in a PR campaign.

An attorney John knew and respected would later take a small chunk for 'dotting the i's and crossing the t's' in a contract worth nine point five million dollars.

By the time we left, I felt Conway had discovered much to admire in John. He has a way of doing that.

She, however, still didn't like me. I found that redeeming.

Outside, the sun, unimpeded by clouds, was glorifying the day.

A day when my friend started the morning broke and ended the afternoon a millionaire.

Jessica and I had made out pretty damn well, too.

Ahh, the unpredictable joys of capitalism.

Nice to be on the receiving end for a change.

Too BIG: Gary Tarulli

11. TO SPEAK OR NOT TO SPEAK

AS THE DAYS PASSED, corporate executives noted what John's immense popularity was doing for Komfort's bottom line. They began to ply him with contract offers. And just like the wild predictions about his potential size, there was no upper limit to what they would do to obtain his product endorsement. It began with a flood of high-dollar offers from big-and-tall clothing stores, home exercise equipment manufacturers, makers of powdered protein shakes, and pharmaceutical companies selling male potency pills.

An endorsement of these products by a person of John's physical stature made some logical sense. Other products, well, not so much. That didn't stop companies from trying. If hawked by John in a splashy ad, wouldn't customers understand the benefit of a deodorant that could last all day? Or the merits of an incredibly tough trash bag? Or perhaps the delights of multi-ply toilet paper so very soft yet impervious to penetration by human hands?

Despite the potential windfall, John could not be swayed. He politely but firmly turned down every enticement. Knowing him as I did, no explanation was needed. By any reasonable measure, he had become wealthy, and his finances were future-proof. His fame gave him the means to earn a boatload of coin whenever necessary.

Nevertheless, the luxury of having a flush bank account while simultaneously being unencumbered by the day-to-day demands of steady employment presented my friend with a new problem:

Now what?

The Squad was assembled to help answer that question and celebrate our recent good fortune.

I picked up Jessica in my now wholly owned EV and proceeded to the mansion, alternately named by me as Demasiado Grande. As we entered, I commented that the door openings were eight feet high instead of the usual seven that accommodate 'the little people.' John passed under them with inches to spare.

"Go ahead, say it," he encouraged. So, I did.

"The door frames here aren't in danger of being splintered by your head."

"You have the writer's gift of pointing out the obvious."

"The real skill is in the embellishment."

"And you never disappoint."

"There they go again, Amanda," Jessica commented, holding stemware and a newly opened bottle of wine. Jessica felt more than comfortable enough to join in the friendly insults. It didn't matter who happened to be the target.

We left the kitchen, skirted two spiral staircases, bypassed a massive living room, and approached the sound of splashing and laughing. Feigning exhaustion from the journey, we exited into the sunshine by passing through the maw of a twenty-foot door. With the mere touch of a finger, successive panels slid aside and stacked onto themselves. No home should be without one.

A heated saltwater pool with a natural rock waterfall and an integral eight-person Jacuzzi sparkled in the midday sun. Jessica and I had obeyed Amanda's command to bring bathing suits. We changed inside the pool's bathhouse and then climbed into the bubbling water. I quickly grokked why the women had been asked to pose nude. When John entered, water sloshed over the side. He smiled, then poured four glasses of a refreshing Vinho Verde.

Brad and Carrie, seeing us, waved from the pool's far end.

"They appear happy," I remarked.

"Kids are quick to adapt," John said. "Their friends are influenced by what their parents think of me, who, in turn, are influenced by what the public thinks of me, which is influenced by social media. For the moment, the prevailing opinion is favorable. Of course, living in the mansion of a recognizable athlete doesn't hurt when it comes to putting a smile on their faces. But you know, there could be a lot more kids in that pool. I have to give mine credit for weeding out the fair-weather kind."

"Do you ever want to return to your former home?" Jessica pointedly asked.

"Eventually ... we'd like to," Amanda responded, surprised at the question's timing.

What Jessica said next may have led to her inquiry. "Since we're all together, I thought this was a good occasion to share a little news. John, you know I've been monitoring your weight and height daily. Both are increasing, but at a significantly slower rate."

We all agreed that was welcome news.

"What does that tell you?" John asked.

Jessica hesitated, then said: "Since no one on the planet knows what's going on with you, the short answer is 'damned if I know.'"

We discussed the implications of John remaining at or near his present quadruple 'x' size, concluding that a future existed where he might lead something approaching a 'normal' life.

Not one to ponder the 'what ifs,' John turned the conversation to the present, seeking our counsel on how to avoid becoming a prisoner in his own home.

"There are limitations," he complained, "on what I can do and where I can go without being troubled by the public. The attention has consequences. I tried resuming my workout at the gym. While I was bench-pressing, a woman—she must have been staring—flew right off her treadmill."

"A stan?" Jess asked.

"Just a fan, I suppose."

"What weight?" I asked.

"One twenty-five, I guess. She was pretty thin." John smiled. "Oh, you mean me? What do I bench? The equivalent of four of her."

All I could say to that was, "Damn."

"She asked me to sign her water bottle with a marker pen. And that's the problem. Everybody wants my autograph. Traffic stops and stares even while I walk to my RV. Good thing Karter installed a workout room in the basement."

"The novelty of seeing you will wear off," Amanda said. "Meanwhile, can I have your autograph?"

"It's right there on the marriage license, honey."

"Any plans?" I asked.

"I've had public speaking offers. I haven't said anything because up until now, I haven't taken the requests too seriously."

"Do any interest you?" Jessica asked.

"A little. There was a request to give a commencement speech at Branford University."

"That's late," Jessica said. "Graduation is only a week from now."

"Their speaker dropped out."

"Who was he?" I asked. "Or she."

"Congressman Julian Hargrove," John responded.

"Sounds familiar," I said, struggling to place the name.

"Hasn't he been in the news lately?" Amanda asked.

"That's who!" I said, remembering. "He might be indicted. I can't recall what for. Sexual assault? Or was it embezzlement?"

"Likely both," Jessica commented, her low opinion of politicians similar to mine.

"The university must have canceled his ass." I grinned at John. "Tough act to follow."

John refreshed our glasses. The wine was kept pleasingly chilled because the hot tub had a built-in cooler and, of course, quad speakers. There was, however, no Alexa to question regarding the specifics of Congressman Hargrove's looming indictment. I'd have to leave a note about that glaring omission in the mansion's complaint box.

"I'm concerned that my physical appearance is the attraction," John said. "And not what I say. That's something I want to avoid."

"I disagree," Amanda protested.

"So do I," Jessica said. "You have quite a lot to say. Recent experiences make you unique."

I chimed in. "Plenty of celebrities, politicians, and marketers spout what they think are pearls of wisdom, earning five figures for as little as twenty minutes. I don't believe Socrates would charge that much if he were alive today."

"Branford's offering $25,000. I don't want their money," John added.

"Donate it back," Jessica suggested. "Then take the write-off."

I watched as a bead of condensation scurried down my cold wine glass. I addressed John. "Not every word has to be dripping with meaning. On occasion, you can be entertaining. If you have difficulty writing a speech, I'm willing to offer a few suggestions; I can be your editor or sounding board."

"Thanks. Wait. Only on occasion?"

"Don't want your ego to become as big as you are."

"Maybe a big ego is necessary when you stand in front of a large audience."

"You have plenty of experience," I said. "You did live TV."

"TV appearances are different."

"Pretend the audience is naked," Jessica suggested.

"Fair is fair, John," Amanda offered. "Women in the audience will be doing that to you."

John groaned. "You're not helping."

"Don't you remember," Amanda volunteered, trying to be helpful, "Jessica's suggestion about public attention?"

"'If you can't beat 'em, join 'em?'" John responded.

"That's the one."

"Treat this the same way ... on your terms. Instead of people coming to you, you go to the people. You decide the who, what, where, and when."

Encouraged, John decided to take our advice. How could he know that his first public speaking gig would trigger a host of unusual events? That's the problem with trying to predict the future, he would say.

12. COMMENCEMENT

AS JOHN PREPARED TO give his commencement speech, I wondered: Does any generation listen to advice from the one that came before? Should they? An expression coined in the nineteen-sixties vainly proclaimed, "Don't trust anyone over thirty." The young adults who lived then are now twice thirty. How can they be trusted if, by prior definition, they can't even trust themselves?

Looking out on a sea of black caps and gowns, I simplified my skepticism. Every generation has the same primary complaint: Your hand-me-down world sucks. Little do they know or care that they will be vilified for attaining the same result. With me short on optimism, it was a good thing that John, not I, was to be the guest speaker.

I had to admit, however, that a more glorious day could not have been scripted. The unusually warm weather that held us hostage during the last several weeks, pushed by a wafting wind, made a welcome retreat. A jumble of puffy clouds, the type that kids fantasize into fanciful shapes, cast their moving shadows on Branford

University's expansive lawn. Beyond, there lay a profusion of colors—the reds, yellows, greens, and oranges of a field of wildly growing late spring flowers. In their midst, I could see Van Gogh standing at his easel.

A thousand folding chairs had been placed on the lawn, each occupied by a newly minted graduate. Nearby, on bleachers, were family and friends, all anxious to see John Whitmore and maybe to hear him speak. In a VIP section sat the members of the media, donors, Amanda, the kids, Jessica, and me.

Thanks to John's notoriety, more people were in attendance than had been formally invited. Some were standing, while others were lying on blankets. The backdrop of sky, the spread of colorful blankets, the pleasant weather, and the energy of a jubilant crowd all contributed to an atmosphere more conducive to a festival than a graduation.

A temporary stage had been erected where dignitaries offered a series of monotonous but mercifully short speeches, mostly tried-and-true platitudes. The class valedictorian, nearly hidden behind the tallest podium that could be found for the occasion, had the honor of introducing the guest speaker.

"We are fortunate," she began tremulously, "to have with us today a man who requires no introduction. That won't stop me anyway. We all recognize him, and it's pretty easy to do, from podcasts and media appearances, which, I think you'd all agree, have been pretty awesome. He's known for being laid-back but doesn't stay back. He doesn't take any BS, and we certainly have witnessed a lot of it thrown his way. He has the rare quality of answering detractors without being condescending or offensive. By action and appearance, he is a man of considerable substance. Graduating class, let us give a warm welcome to John Whitmore!"

To thunderous applause, John rose from where he had been sitting. He approached the podium where, with an object in hand, the valedictorian was ready with a few final words.

"Thank you, Mr. Whitmore, so very much for accepting our

invitation to speak on such short notice. The people in the audience should know that you, unlike the person who may have been standing here, have waived the speaking fee Branford University offers. For this reason, and one a bit more obvious, we'd like to distinguish you with our honorary 'Big Man on Campus' award."

"Thank you!" John shouted over applause and laughter. Smiling, he held up a splendid cut-glass pyramid for the crowd to see. 'I'd very much like to say that this beautiful award has left me speechless, but as it happens, I have one right here." John reached into his suit pocket to hold up what I knew to be the barest outline of the remarks he was about to make. He paused, waiting for the cheers and laughter to subside before resuming.

"Hello, everyone! What a beautiful day! A time to savor being alive and to celebrate the achievements of these graduates traveling through the prime of their lives. Congratulations, we say to all of you! You did it!"

John again waited for the cheering to stop before resuming.

"But what, exactly, have you done?

Some say you have earned passage into the 'real world.' There may be some truth to it. You've been living with people your age, sharing many of the same interests, cares, and aspirations. For most of you, that is about to change in a big way. You will have to make adjustments.

And yet, something about that phrase is insulting.

The real world?

Is there some other world you've been in that the rest of us are unaware of?

Nonsense! From birth, our trials and tribulations, joys, pains, setbacks, and accomplishments have happened in the 'real' world. For all of us, with no exception! I choose not to denigrate what you have experienced in the last four years and certainly not in the previous twenty.

We've all heard yet another statement: 'Youth is wasted on the young.'

You can thank George Bernard Shaw for that one.

I doubt it's true, but my advice is simple:

Stop getting wasted!"

A raucous laugh erupted as the intentional double meaning of John's remark sank in.

"But wait, there's more! For you Gen Z'ers out there, more insults are lobbed your way. I'm sure you've heard most of them:

That you're entitled.

Need instant gratification.

Have zero attention span.

Lack social skills.

Are lazy.

And then, after repeatedly throwing shade your way, they accuse you of having low self-esteem!

LOL! Laugh—it's funny.

Some try to bait you into being angry. I've seen my share of haters. According to those supermarket tabloids, my lovely wife has wanted to divorce me three separate times."

"That's four times, sweetheart!" Amanda shouted out. "But who's counting?!"

"Laugh," John called out as laughter traveled through the crowd. "Laugh, and you discover the best way to beat them! Laugh precisely because those in politics and elsewhere prefer you to be angry. Angry at trans. At Muslims. Jews. Christians. Liberals. Conservatives. Atheists. Angry at anyone who doesn't believe as they do. Why? A psych major will tell you that angry people don't think straight. A poly sci major will say that unreasoned anger creates divisions that the devious thrive on. Both are ways to divide and conquer by people with a cult following or who crave power.

My advice? If you don't already have one, cultivate a sense of humor. You'll certainly need one in this absurd world! A cray-cray world where a proposed commencement speaker, a person likely facing indictment, could have presented himself as an inspirational role model to you, the promise of America's future. He might have been speaking at this podium, articulating clever things. The words may have sounded believable. But is the man?

People like him typify one thing perfectly: one of your generation's greatest challenges—and one we all share. It's that of separating truth from lies, facts from fiction.

How, you might ask?

By listening to everyone.

But let no one preach to you.

By having empathy for others.

But let no one tell you how to feel.

By having faith in someone or something.

By first having faith in yourself.

You can meet these challenges by reaching out with an open hand.

Be it big..."

John held up an impressive hand, fingers spread, for the audience to admire.

"...or small. Male or female. Straight or gay. Young or old. Or any such dichotomy, real or imagined, that can be named. You can do far more good in this world with an open hand than a clenched fist. With an open hand, a cell phone is impossible to hold... and often, that can be a good thing.

Looking out in the distance, over that field, we don't see the obvious challenges that past generations have confronted and mastered. No mastodons to hunt, continents to explore, or world wars to fight. No, the challenges you face are more insidious. For that reason, they may be more daunting. What are the ethical limits of genetic engineering? How do you prepare for a pandemic? What are the consequences of artificial intelligence? How do we deal with global warming? How do you rescue a tattered democracy?

Now is your time to make a change. No one said it would be easy. Do not obsess about a bleak future. Live in the now. That is where the wonder resides. Yes, the last four years of education have burdened you with debt. I'm not saying that's fair. Is a family bankrupted because they lack health insurance fair? Is the fact that every generation, including yours and mine, has trampled the environment fair? Is a political system corrupted by partisan politics, bad actors, and special interests fair? Hear what I'm saying. Don't expect pity. Don't *expect* the government to act in your best interest. Not when self-serving politicians are in office.

Refuse to let these fools get under your skin. Vote them out! Remove them like an unwanted tattoo. Perhaps the name of an ex-lover?!"

The peals of laughter gave a young woman the courage to yell, "You hearin' that, Greg?!" which produced even more laughter.

"Do you believe," John resumed, "that your vote has no meaning? It has diminished meaning. But like the benefit of compound interest, the more you vote, the more meaning accrues. From my vantage point, I see a thousand potential votes—with concerted effort, enough to influence a local House of Representatives election.

The world is full of challenges. Pick one. Immerse yourself in a worthy cause or occupation. At first, the task may appear insurmountable. Don't despair—inspire! Tap into what you have in abundance: your fresh viewpoint and youthful vitality. Individuals exactly like yourselves are what give us all hope for the future."

With one long arm, John pointed out into the distance.

"So, I encourage you to take a harder look out there. *See* the beautiful day. One by one, more days like this will unfold. Blossoming like the flowers in that field.

Promise and potential!

What you will see out there is the rest of your life!"

As John left the podium, a thousand grads rose and cheered. As he entered the VIP section, he was welcomed by hugs from

Amanda, Jessica, Brad, and Carrie. It was gratifying to see how proud the kids were of their dad.

I congratulated my friend on being very much more than occasionally entertaining. The speech was effective—an appropriate balance of optimism and realism for the uninitiated youth facing the troubles of a brave new world.

One small surprise was that John chose not to ignore his size but instead used it to his advantage.

Before the speech, my friend showed me his notes. What he wrote down was no more than an outline. I had found that both disconcerting and amazing. Much of what he said was either committed to memory or extemporaneous. He must have had a superb feel for the moment.

There was more emphasis on politics than I expected. Predictably, the news media repeatedly ran clips and commented on those portions. Although his name was never directly mentioned, this did not go over well at Representative Julian Hargrove's headquarters.

For his election opponent, it raised eyebrows and presented an opportunity.

Too BIG: Gary Tarulli

13. THE PERFECT TRIFECTA

SOON AFTER JOHN'S COMMENCEMENT SPEECH, he received a call from Joshua Greene, the campaign manager for Gunther Jackson, who was running for Congress. The call, a request to "meet-and-greet" the candidate, came out of the blue, but the real purpose of the sit-down was crystal: Jackson would be seeking John's public endorsement.

As a candidate, Jackson had a few issues going against him. He was Black and gay and running as an Independent—the perfect trifecta in ways to lose an election. One additional handicap had so far gone unnoticed: he considered himself an agnostic. No one—not the media, his opponent, or the voting public—cared because Jackson was twenty-plus points behind in the latest polls.

His opponent, to borrow another sports term, had scored a hat trick by being white, straight, and a Christian Conservative. He also benefited from his electable good looks, a war chest bursting with funding from special interest groups, and being the incumbent.

He did, however, have one festering problem: He was under investigation for campaign finance violations and embezzlement. When you have the ethics of a scoundrel, a potential indictment does nothing to dissuade you from running for office. Judging by the polls, his supporters wholeheartedly agreed. We know this person to be Julian Hargrove, the same personage John obliquely referenced in his commencement speech.

The prospect of helping to unseat Hargrove was mighty tempting. Still, John had other concerns and was disinclined to dip his very big toe into the polluted pool of politics. He and I had a pragmatic approach to the dark art of voting. We tended to use an imaginary scorecard to grade a candidate. No politician checked off all the right boxes on critical issues, and even the correct answers were subject to erasure once the person was elected. In the final analysis, the choices often stunk, but we held our noses and made them.

Based on his stated positions, Jackson appeared to be a substantially better choice than most. An in-person chat would perhaps be more revealing. On that basis, his request for a sit-down was reluctantly accepted and scheduled. Naturally, the Squad was reconvened. Collectively, we would subject the candidate to our unique style of vetting.

We greeted Jackson and his campaign manager at the front door. When people meet my friend for the first time, they understandably tend to be awed by his size. Not so much Jackson, even though the man was a couple of inches shorter than average. As the two shook hands, he looked up and said: "If I could average our heights, we'd both be better off."

"I'd avoid making that a campaign promise," John suggested, smiling.

"Wouldn't think of it," Jackson said, returning the smile. "This is Joshua Greene, my good friend and campaign manager."

After obligatory intros and handshakes, Jackson asked, "And who are these two delights?"

"Brad and Carrie," Amanda said. "Not sure about the 'delights.'"

"Sticking around for a civics lesson?"

"You read my mind," Amanda responded. "But I doubt they'll sit still. Please follow me; we can all sit comfortably in the sunroom."

As we passed through the intervening rooms, Jessica whispered in my ear, "Greene looks like that actor-rapper 50 Cent, only a tad bigger with a fuller beard."

"Think of him as 60 Cents," I offered.

In the center of the sunroom, forming an open-ended square, were three expensive overstuffed sofas and a not-so-subtle reminder of whose home we were in—a giant coffee table whose entire top was made of glass etched into the pattern and texture of a basketball. Beams of filtered light reaching the terrazzo floor prompted Jackson to look at the ceiling. We politely chuckled when he observed that the room had more glass than a Gothic church.

"Before we delve into why you're here," John began, "we'd like to hear your stance on some of the issues."

"Fair enough. We anticipated as much," Greene replied for Jackson. He reached into a black leather briefcase and gave each of us a handout. "That's a summary of our positions."

Once again, I assumed the role of an attack dog. I quickly scanned the handout and made a point of tossing it aside. "All well and good," I said, "but if there is anyone less trustworthy than a politician, it would be a politician running for office."

John gave me the bemused look I've come to know well. "Be prepared," he said. "Max can be threatening when off leash."

"Oh, it's quite all right," Jackson replied. "I'm not put off. Rather, I completely agree, though I would suggest that, as for mistrust, telemarketers give congressmen a run for their money. About me, Max, how can I relieve you of that mindset?"

"Can you, though?" I asked. "I've a low opinion of people, and most of the time I don't have to apologize because they tend to prove me right." I locked eyes on Jackson. "So, tell us, what skeletons are hiding in your closet?"

"I emptied my closet a long time ago," Jackson replied, staring back. "The only thing to come out of it was me."

"Good answer," I said. But pit bulls refuse to let go. "Nothing else?"

"Nothing comes to mind," Jackson replied, thinking. His expression turned somber. "Keep this between us. I would be embarrassed if anyone saw the gold-colored hammer pants I still own."

"And you should be," Jessica said, laughing.

"What's a hammer pant, Mom?" Carrie asked, finally having her curiosity piqued.

"Something a clown might look good in, sweetheart."

"Speaking of which," John said, "what do you think of Hargrave?"

"My sources say he's dirty," Jackson replied. "But leaving that aside, if you don't want trans using a public bathroom, he's your man."

"You would be in favor of a transsexual woman entering a lady's restroom?" Jessica asked, pretending to be offended. She gave me a wink. "Whatever is next? Participation in women's sports?"

She and I, as I shall later explain, already had 'The Talk.' I knew she was testing Jackson. My guess was he was sharp enough to know, too.

"Government has far better things to do, don't you think?" he asked. "Besides, ladies' restrooms have no urinals, so if there is anything left to see, exactly who's seeing it? Think on it."

We did. Due to Jackson's careful wording, the children didn't have to.

"You're at risk of being called woke," John commented.

"Wouldn't be true, and don't care. I've been marked with more labels than a department store. As for trans women in sports," Jackson continued, "again, this shouldn't be a federal matter. Personally, however, I would say I don't like the idea. They would have an unfair competitive advantage."

While the adults were wasting time gabbing about where trans could take a piss, Amanda paid close attention to her kids' reaction. Seeing none, she asked them directly: "Do you have any trans friends?"

She received a one-word answer: "Probably."

And that said it all—her youngsters couldn't care less. It's we adults who complicate matters. Bored with the grown-ups' civics lesson, the kids asked to be excused and rocketed out the side door.

"I'd like to hear," Amanda said, "your thoughts on abortion."

That didn't take long, I thought. Jackson took a deep breath before replying: "Unfortunately, I'm compelled to have one, aren't I?"

"I'm afraid I don't get your meaning," Amanda said.

"Men shouldn't be deciding such an intensely personal issue for a woman. Government, for the most part, shouldn't either, and largely didn't until the 1860s. Religion has co-opted ethical considerations, and this shouldn't be in a supposedly secular country. On the other hand, where do you draw the line if you believe the government has become too big and intrusive? If you want to curb the size and role of government, you shouldn't expect that government to pay for abortion except, perhaps, when the woman's life is in real danger and she has no income."

"A poor woman denied an abortion," Amanda rejoined, "is ultimately far more costly to the government."

"I've seen the numbers," Jackson replied. "I'm attempting to be logically consistent. A person who believes abortion is murder will never agree to any form of government funding. You can't expect them to."

"When a poor woman, maybe she's on Public Assistance, has an unwanted baby, she will never climb out of poverty."

"Never? Listen, my personal feelings may more closely align with yours. But there are times, and I consider this one, when those feelings get in the way of approaching a highly contentious issue. Think of it strategically. By taking the issue of government funding away, you undermine one of the abortion foes' arguments. No? I can see from your expression that my position will likely make you unhappy. So be it. I didn't come here expecting to make everyone happy."

Jackson was right about that. As time progressed, we did not agree with him on everything; how could we, since we didn't always agree among ourselves? At least his responses were reasoned. We asked for and received his insights concerning the military ("way too big"), Social Security ("stupid bastards will wait for it to go bankrupt before doing anything"), the environment ("if we keep it up, we'll all be eating Soylent Green. Pity the vegans.").

Jackson, resignation on his face, addressed us. "If I'm elected, can I solve any of these problems? There are four hundred and thirty-four other voices in the House. I'll be the stranger in a strange land."

"You could quote Lincoln," John suggested. "'A house divided against itself cannot stand.'"

Mercifully, I thought, Jessica and I weren't divided. We had successfully completed 'The Talk.' In the past, it concerned couples' feelings about having children. That ship had sailed and disappeared beyond the horizon for Jess and me. Or it might have concerned personal thoughts about marriage.

Today, 'The Talk" is about the contentious issues of the day and your partner's political persuasion. That conversation has become commonplace, maybe essential, because we live in a divided country where disagreements may end a romantic relationship or result in divorce. 'The Talk' may not happen all at once, but it happens, so you might as well get it over with.

I had started daydreaming, mesmerized by the shifting light patterns on the stone floor. Jessica, her warm leg next to mine, nudged me awake.

As he often did, John listened more than spoke. He addressed Jackson. "You're here seeking my endorsement," he began, "which I am willing to give, subject to one condition. Actually, two." Grinning, he then glanced my way. "One is for Max."

I had no idea what my friend was up to.

"You have our attention," Greene said.

"Condition one: Max has writing creds. I would like him to compose one of those minute-long political spots you run, but to improve upon the type of ad people have come to hate."

"What?!" Greene exclaimed, making motions to leave. "No way..."

Jackson placed a hand on his campaign manager's shoulder to stop him. "I'm intrigued, Josh. We should hear him out."

"Second condition," John went on, "is that the ad is run with full exposure, not buried in a graveyard slot somewhere."

"How can we possibly accept that?" Jackson protested. "It would amount to giving Max free rein to say anything, anything at all, on my behalf."

"I'm good with that," I said, intrigued by the possibility of putting words in a politician's mouth.

"Max writes the spot," John insisted. "If you don't like it, don't use it. But if you choose not to, I will not endorse you publicly."

Greene shook his head. Jackson, however, was clever enough to propose another idea.

"Why not have Max write your endorsement? We'll make that the political spot."

"No. For two reasons. I'll write my own. And I also believe Max can help your campaign."

Jackson turned to his campaign manager. "What do you think, Josh? You onboard with this?"

Josh needed to stroke his beard to think. He probably grew a beard for that very reason. "We're down twenty in the polls," he conceded. "We need to try something. You won't reconsider, John?"

"No."

"The commencement speech may have already helped you," Amanda advised them. "Two days ago, you were down twenty-four points."

"You'll get sixty seconds," Jackson said, consenting to the idea with a half-smile. "After all, how much damage can you do in sixty seconds?"

"I guess you'll just have to wait and see," I said. My smile was a full shit-eating grin, even with only a vague idea of the verbal mischief I could concoct.

Jackson and Greene departed, hurrying to the day's third campaign stop, a fundraiser.

Babies to kiss in the morning, asses to kiss in the evening. All in a day's work.

We stayed in and ordered Chinese.

14. ENDORSEMENT

JESSICA'S CONDO IS DOUBLE-PLUS the size of mine; it's too big and twice as expensive. We were tangled together on her sofa, wasting life watching addictive YouTube videos, forcing me to keep the remote handy to skip the annoying commercials. I dislike commercials. Politicians even more, and now I was expected to create a commercial for a politician.

"Do you know there are one hundred eighty words in a sixty-second commercial?" I asked. "Give or take."

"Not very many," Jessica returned. "But they can be important words."

"You bought into Jackson's rap?"

"He's different from most. I'm going to take him at his word."

"Risky."

"Not overly," she said, slowly unbuttoning my shirt, "I'm a good judge of character. Why else would you be lying on my sofa?"

Later, with my laptop in front of me, I recalled Jessica's words: "He's different from most." When I asked, "How so?" she had trouble replying, finally saying that he seemed more contained within himself, a bit self-deprecating, unlike the typical politician running off at the mouth.

In a small way, he was similar to my friend, who preferred not to draw undue attention to himself. Jackson, however, desperately needed publicity to close an almost insurmountable gap in the polls.

I began typing. The *only* way to make this work was to create a disturbance in the force. If I could, the media would replay the paid-for spot several times, giving Jackson free exposure.

Writing quickly (overthinking meant overediting), I came up with the following. I wondered if Jackson had the nerve to accept it.

I'm Gunther Jackson, and I'm running for Congress.

Why should you vote for me and not the other guy? Because somewhere deep inside, you realize a person's character matters. Shame on you if you don't know this, and doubly shame on you if you refuse to vote out of laziness, or despair, or because you consider yourself too damn busy. They're the excuses of a defeatist.

Is that you?!

So, you've become pessimistic by listening to the news and seeing constant BS in Congress. You're probably thinking the ship of state we're passengers on is too far gone. That the breach in the hull is too big. I get the feeling. But consider this: To save your ass, wouldn't you rather get a bucket and start bailing than go down with the ship?

Some of my opponent's supporters, aiming to defeat and divide us, point out that I'm Black and gay. I'd make no more of it than describing them as white and straight. In either case, who gives a damn? You should only care that I'm never going to divide us. And I'll damn well never be a defeatist. Not while running for office, where I'm going to kick serious butt, and not when I win and represent you in Congress.

Don't be distracted by the sideshow you see in the media. Subtract all the nonsense. Look past the smoke and mirrors. You'll find my opponent standing there with nothing to offer.

As for me, it's simple. All you have to do is open your cell or laptop and examine my position on the issues.

And then, put down that damn cellphone and vote.

I self-edited a sentence that described Jackson's opponent in a way that would make a longshoreman blush. Jessica also didn't like the line, "Stop jerking off in your parents' basement," telling me it was offensive. When I changed "basement" to "attic," she liked it even less. I was forced to agree, even though young males don't turn out to vote in representative numbers.

I gave John a copy of the text to read. From him, I earned a small amount of praise and a comment: "You know, Max, that getting involved like this, by writing these words, you're proving yourself to be a valuable member of society."

"Well," I said, "you don't have to go and insult me."

Later, upon reflecting on John's exact words, it dawned on me that my getting involved was his aim from the very start. Member of society or not, I had exercised, for me, restraint. Jackson reluctantly agreed to do the spot. On the day of taping, he overcame his hesitancy; he was "all-in," and his energetic delivery made my words more colorful. The ad turned out to be very effective but not nearly so much as John's endorsement, which (see below) occurred the following day:

I'm John Whitmore, and I'm endorsing Gunter Jackson for Congress.

I have spoken with him. I have closely examined his record. In doing so, I have come to believe he has an approach to the issues that is compassionate and insightful. In every way possible, he represents a clear choice over that other guy. Equally important, he has earned my trust.

Like you, however, I have witnessed politicians abuse that trust. When this occurs, we often have no recourse. Fortunately, I do. To the extent my endorsement has an appreciable effect, so can its withdrawal, which, you can be assured, I would make public. Do I have an expectation of this being necessary? Absolutely not. I make this pledge because I value the faith many of you have in me.

My endorsement of Gunther Jackson today is not given lightly. I feel compelled to do so because he is not only the better candidate.

He is the better man.

And that matters.

The political pundits could not remember anyone making an endorsement while simultaneously threatening to retract it. "Huge misstep by Mr. Whitmore and the candidate!" headlines pronounced. Jackson, too, was surprised by John's statement and wondered if he'd see any benefit.

Three days later, the wonks and pundits were proven wrong, though they were able to bury their misjudgment beneath jargon like 'gaffe,' 'coffers,' 'stumping,' 'dark horse,' 'bellwether state,' 'battleground state,' 'blue state,' 'red state,' 'purple state,' etc. What they had failed to realize was that John's unusual statement enhanced an already stellar reputation for honesty. His endorsement and the political spot I authored became wildly successful. Within a week, the hoped-for bump in the polls materialized, resulting in an ecstatic Jackson surging to within three points of his opponent.

A worried Hargrave had always considered the public as fickle as the participants on 'The Bachelorette.' A politician for most of his adult life, he understood just how easily voter sentiment could be swayed. All it took was one slip of the tongue or one news story, true or fabricated. Why play fair when you're forced to court the public? The trick is to make your constituents (which, to him, meant voters) believe you're a stand-up guy.

Experience told him exactly when and how to use that rose hidden behind his back.

15. SECULAR INQUISITION

HARGRAVE WAS A HOUSE Armed Services Committee (HASC) member, a governmental body known to almost no one. But that would change. As Chairman of that body's Intelligence and Special Operations subcommittee, he convinced members of his party to issue subpoenas to John and 'parties of interest,' compelling them to answer questions, some potentially embarrassing, concerning the 'big man's' unique capabilities and potential.

Hargrave's underlying motive was to woo voters away from his opponent by using the committee's public forum to weaken John's image, thereby mitigating the value of his recent endorsement. Additionally, Jackson's ability to judge a person's character, a skill a politician is presumed to need, would be called into question. In other words, guilt by association—or as Hargrave crudely put it: "Stand next to an outhouse, you get stink on you."

The charade, if not having a likelihood of success, would at least act as a public distraction. Not wanting to lose a seat in a closely divided House, the members of Hargrave's party were supportive.

They presented the idea as originating from the committee, so no one could accuse the congressman of being politically motivated. Going one step further, he took a subordinate seat and relegated witness questioning to a fellow committee member, Vivian Verte, a sometimes conspiracy theorist well known for speaking her mind. She was the perfect choice since the underlying aim was to throw as much shit against the wall as possible to see what would stick.

The orchestration gained traction when the committee learned that the Defense Department had one unblinking eye on John from the beginning. Why? Stories had surfaced that the Chinese were conducting genetic experiments intending to create a supersoldier. A solitary seven-and-a-half-foot John would hardly be a convincing counterthreat, but an entire battalion?! Officials at the Pentagon had no concept of how or if this supersoldier from the pages of a Marvel comic book could be created, but the prospect made it to the drawing boards.

John's attendance caused the media to hype the hearing, and a crowd had amassed in front of the hearing building. As our Squad attempted to enter, a man suddenly stepped out from the line of reporters and rushed at Amanda, saying, "You're the bitch married to this big asshole."

The man, who had the powerful build of a weightlifter, towered above everyone in the crowd except John. The immediacy of the situation dictated what happened next, and what had happened took five seconds—or half a lifetime, depending on your concept of space-time.

John had remarkable strength and agility. A rush of adrenaline made him stronger and faster. In a blur of motion, he blocked the attacker's approach. Then, grasping the man's shirt with one massive hand, he elevated him high off the ground, where he hung suspended like a bunch of grapes on a vine. The man didn't stay skyward long, for he was thrown bodily into the crowd of reporters, parting them like the Red Sea. John had the presence of mind to ask Amanda if she was okay. The answer was not only evident from her appearance, but she had not been idle during the altercation, having shouted after the man, "Sure, turn tail and run, you cowardly fuck!"

Unfortunately, Jessica and I could do little more than watch, and the man slipped away in the confusion. After a brief period of pushing and shoving, the four of us were ushered by security into the building. Upon learning what happened, the committee wisely decided to delay the main event until the following day.

The incident took place so rapidly that eyewitness descriptions (and there were dozens of them) were laughably unreliable. That didn't matter. The attacker was apprehended within hours when several of his associates identified him from media footage that supplanted less newsworthy stories concerning the record number of 110-degree days, grain shortages causing famine, and a protracted war somewhere.

Postponement of the hearing provided the Squad time to discuss what transpired.

"What stands out in my mind," Jessica offered, "was the measured, almost calm way the man hurled his profanity at you. You'd think if the bastard were so upset, he would have made more of a point of it by screaming."

We agreed. Nothing about the situation should have evoked composure. It almost seemed as if the words had been scripted.

"Amanda did all the yelling," I said. "You could scare the spots off a lion."

"Lions don't have spots."

"Making it even more impressive."

"The man has no record," Jessica said. "He's already represented by an attorney who is stating his client will plead guilty for no jail time."

"Interesting," John said, thinking. "We should entertain the possibility that he was a plant, though I'm not sure what would be gained."

Since none of this 'evidence' appeared conclusive, John laid the matter to rest. The next day, it was reawakened. By me.

Coverage of the prior day's excitement increased the media's coverage of the HASC Sub-Committee hearing. Public interest, which already had 'legs,' now grew arms, torso, and head—a Frankenstein monster stitched together to generate higher ratings (AKA, higher ad revenue) and, incidentally, to inform the public. Livestreaming expanded to millions. The main event occurred in a large governmental meeting room—envision leather, wood, and painted portraits—bursting at the seams with the public and press.

John, Amanda, Jessica, and I, microphones situated in front of us, had the premium front-row seats. A GS-1 pay-grade federal employee had carved out a space large enough for my friend, who appeared relaxed and comfortable. I never expected otherwise. He would sit back, let people play their games, and enjoy the show.

Congresswoman Verte took center stage and kicked off the proceedings. During the swearing-in, I immediately got on her bad side by requesting that a secular phrase be substituted for the 'so help me God' language. "The purpose of this hearing," she began, "is to see if there is good reason to open a preliminary investigation into the origin of this man's disorder and, in doing so, determine the extent of any benefit to the Armed Forces of the United States."

"I can save you the trouble. There isn't," Amanda said. "Hearing adjourned!"

In the bleacher section behind us, people started laughing. I was happy to hear it because I would need all the audience support I could get. Verte ignored the disturbance and plodded ahead. "I understand, Mrs. Whitmore, that you were involved in an unfortunate incident outside this building."

"If you call being assaulted unfortunate, oh yes."

"But you were uninjured?"

"Nary a scratch, Congresswoman, thanks to my husband here. But everyone knows that. Where in heaven's name do you get your news?"

"Well, mostly from you nowadays. You and your famous husband *are* the news."

"If only that weren't true, Congresswoman," Amanda said, turning partway in her chair to gaze at the spectators behind her. "These folks are here at *your* invitation."

"Well, no, at this committee's invitation, and for a good reason," Verte shot back. "I have a question for you, Mr. Whitmore. Is it true that you lifted this so-called attacker bodily and hurled him into a group of reporters?"

"Had to," John replied. "Out of necessity."

"Would you say you did this impulsively, without regard to the safety of the people present?"

"I'd say I took exactly the right amount of time to protect my wife."

"Thank you, honey," Amanda yelled out, grinning. "You're the best."

"You're welcome, sweetheart. Anytime."

"All joking aside," Verte said, ignoring the audience's laughter and forcing a smile. "What you did yesterday, Mr. Whitmore, would take a great deal of strength, would it not?"

"There may have been a bit of adrenaline involved."

Unsatisfied with the answer, Verte turned her attention to Jessica, who verified her medical credentials in detail, along with her recent assignment as John's personal physician.

"Very impressive," Verte said impatiently. "What I'm trying to get at here is that Mr. Whitmore is exceptionally strong for his size."

"That is not correct," Jessica replied. "John is not strong *for* his size. He is as strong *as* his size."

"Is there a difference?" Verte said, appearing confused.

"Of course, and I'll explain. His strength is commensurate with his size. If his strength were unusual for his size, we'd have two medical mysteries to solve. One has been quite enough, thank you."

"I see," Verte said dismissively. Judging from the Congresswoman's confused expression, there was a better-than-even chance she did not see at all. "Nevertheless," she continued, "he is far stronger than the average man, wouldn't you say?"

Jessica thought for a moment. "Yes, but to be clear, we are talking..."

"...in that case," Verte interrupted.

Rudeness was never going to work on Jessica. "Excuse me, Congresswoman," she said. "I don't appreciate being cut off mid-sentence. I'd like to finish."

"By all means, go ahead."

"Go ahead, *Doctor*," Jessica insisted. "I've referred to you as Congresswoman. You've yet to address me by my title. I was attempting to make a distinction concerning relative strength. If you intend to find a responsible chemical or biological agent—and I assume that is your aim—that would be a complete waste of time."

"In your opinion, Doctor," Verte said.

"In my expert opinion, Congresswoman."

"You're a close friend to Mr. Whitmore, aren't you?" Verte resumed, implying that the association could affect the doctor's judgment.

In response, Jessica rattled off ten single-digit numbers.

"And what, pray tell, is that?" Verte asked.

"The phone number of County Central Hospital. I suggest you call them. They have studied John extensively. They have the same professional opinion as I do. And, Congresswoman, I don't believe they and John are close friends."

"All well and good," Verte replied, undaunted. "So, you'd have no objection to further studies being done by medical experts of our choosing?"

"That's not my decision to make, is it?"

John covered his microphone as I did mine, then leaned in and whispered with a half-smile: "Nothing seems to faze her," to which I responded, "I'll give it a try."

"Mr. Whitmore," Verte plodded on, "according to Doctor Merriwether, the crux of the matter is you're just too big."

"That's not what she said. From my perspective, Congresswoman. I'm exactly the right size."

"And from the military's point of view, you could be a valuable asset."

"In what way?"

"Isn't it obvious? The secret could be used if science can determine what caused your affliction. That would be a huge service to the country, don't you think? Why would you be against that?"

"Well, first off, I have no wish to be labeled an asset. How would my worth be calculated? Would I be worth more or less than the five billion wasted on uniforms that the Army never used?"

"Much more," Verte said. To this day, I still ask myself: Was that the dumbest reply to a question I've ever heard? Somehow, John was able to respond.

"They say, Congresswoman, that crazy is doing the same thing repeatedly while expecting different results. The way you answered, crazy is doing the same foolish thing over and over and *not* expecting different results."

That took me a minute to digest. Verte appeared befuddled. She changed tactics.

"Would you say, Mr. Whitmore, that science has yet to diagnose what's going on with you?"

"True enough."

"And, as far as we know, in the whole world, you are the only one to whom this has happened? You are one of a kind. Wouldn't you consider yourself a miracle?"

"I wouldn't want a shrine built for me."

"Damn it, John," I said, "what the hell am I going to do with the four million tons of granite I ordered?"

Over the audience's laughter, I was reprimanded. I hadn't

behaved this badly since kindergarten.

"Obviously, you're not a religious man," Verte continued. "Are you, Mr. Whitmore?"

"My beliefs are not the proper subject of inquiry."

"Your public records are. It's telling that there are no church documents for baptisms or communions for your children. You were married by a Justice of the Peace, not an ordained priest."

"All that is true."

"So, the answer would be that you're not religious."

"There are more than a billion Muslims in the world. Five hundred million followers of Buddhism."

"So you're a Buddhist?"

"Not necessarily. I'm just pointing out the flaw in your logic. You don't have to be a Christian to be religious."

I tried to stifle a laugh but failed. The Congresswoman, increasingly annoyed, was not happy with my deportment. I was now fair game for her ire.

"Is there any purpose whatsoever in your being here today?" she asked me, scowling.

"I get that a lot, hanging around John."

"Just 'hanging around,' you say? You were there when Mrs. Whitmore was attacked. You did nothing?"

"Discretion, they say, is the better part of valor."

"And you were so very discreet," Amanda, grinning, inserted. She, too, had to be reprimanded. I decided then and there to defend Amanda and John the best way I could: by making shit up. Not entirely made up, mind you. A good conspiracy theory, which I knew the Congresswoman to be a devotee of, must contain a smattering of relevant facts. I'd start with those and end with a flourish.

"Congresswoman Verte," I innocently began, "I feel obligated to make this committee aware of my impressions concerning the attempted assault on Mrs. Whitmore. As you have properly pointed out, I was there."

"You have our attention. I remind you, however, that you are still under oath."

"Happily," I said. I then proceeded to describe the attempted assault on Amanda, emphasizing how the attacker happened to be a very imposing man, that his tone of voice lacked anger, and that there was something in his demeanor that did not match the vehemence of his words. Although directed at Amanda, the words seemed designed to provoke John. I pointed out that the attack was conducted in full public view, in a crowd, with little hope of success. I described how quickly the man had been caught and then 'lawyered up.' With the facts out of the way, I gave my opinion. You can do that under oath.

"All this leads me to believe the attack was not what it seemed."

"What are you suggesting?" Verte asked, confused.

"That the attack was premeditated."

"Well, well, what a brilliant conclusion," Verte said, her voice dripping with sarcasm.

"'Yes, premeditated!' I said, almost shouting. "But by whom!?"

Perhaps I've watched too many episodes of 'Law and Order,' but my theatrics had the desired effect. The audience uproar took minutes to subside despite Verte's efforts. When the clamor finally stopped, she was compelled to ask obvious questions.

"You believe someone directed the man to attack? That's absurd. Who? Why?" I believed she did not know the answers. Or maybe she couldn't resist hearing a good conspiracy.

"It's like this," I said, pretending, in part, I knew what 'it' was. "If John had not acted, he'd be branded a coward. If he overreacted, he'd be considered a sadistic brute. Either way, his image would be damaged."

"And, pray tell, what would be gained by that?"

"If you damage John's reputation, you also lessen the value of any political endorsements he might make."

I volunteered no more, leaving others to weigh the

implications. One such person, sitting across from me, was Hargrave. I watched as his face froze and his body stiffened. A Madame Tussauds likeness would have been more animated. When he finally melted, the committee members of his party huddled. After speaking in hushed terms, they adjourned the hearing to the following day. Overnight in our Washington, DC, hotel room, we learned the adjournment had been made permanent.

My mini-tirade had caught Amanda and Jessica by surprise. Not so much John, who was no longer surprised by anything I did or said. He didn't disapprove of my actions, nor would he.

As I've been saying all along, he was, and is, my friend.

16. STRANGE BEDFELLOWS

THE ABSENCE OF VERIFIABLE FACTS does nothing to kill a conspiracy theory. They exist as waifs that thrive on nothingness. Perhaps that is why my yarn involving Hargrave, a verbal stew of fact and supposition, was ultimately short-lived.

My public outburst had a residual effect, giving the Congressman something unsavory to chew on. Slipping in the polls, he desperately needed to create a new election narrative. Being of no moral fiber, he had no qualms about cooking one up, a full-page ad featuring an image of Jackson and John together, with Jackson awkwardly trying to embrace the much taller man. Below the picture was a caption, "Non-Believer Kissing Up." The body of the ad stated that neither man was a churchgoer and lamented their lack of character and absence of faith. The close hug of the two men intimated homosexuality.

The photo, an AI deepfake, was doubly odd because the two men had never embraced and were never seen together in public. Pointing out the deception by the Jackson campaign had little effect. To some, doubting a photograph is akin to questioning your image in a mirror.

Hargrave had given the ad the green light. Trampling the truth and giving offense never stops a politician running scared in an election. They explain away their immoral transgressions with catchphrases such as "desperate times call for desperate measures" and "the end justifies the means."

The low moral standards set by many politicians, combined with the principle of the separation of church and state, should make politics and religion strange, if not unwilling, bedfellows. But this is not always the case. A controversial reverend had begun to use the power of the pulpit to urge his flock to vote for Hargrave.

John knew Jackson to be the better of the two candidates and, more than ever, was intent on helping him. "What are the chances of us changing the Rev's mind?" he asked me.

"Close to zero. Maybe a negative number."

"Spoken like a true skeptic. Do you remember what I said at the start of this madness?"

"'You'd roll with it, or it rolls over you?' A classic. I wrote it down. What do you suggest?"

"Let's have a little fun. I'll invite the man to tea, and we'll have a go at him."

"You think he'll come?"

"Oh, he'll come. He's an evangelist. A bit of a Bible-thumper. He'll try to bring me into the fold, believing others will follow." "

"So he's the sheepdog; you're the pied piper."

"That's the spirit."

The Reverend did come. Like a moth to a flame. We watched

from the vestibule as he exited from a jet-black limo. His driver stayed behind.

The Rev was a serious-looking man in his thirties, younger than I expected, and snappily dressed in a beige suit. I was disappointed he wasn't garbed head-to-toe in black like that priest from *The Omen*. I expressed my dismay to John.

"Same," my friend agreed. "I was hoping to see him perform your exorcism."

"The thought makes my head spin."

The man looked at John carefully, then briefly, at me. I tried not to be the extraneous figure most people considered me to be. One way of doing this was by making observations.

On closer inspection, the Rev's beige suit appeared Italian, perhaps an Armani—not a brand you'd buy as two-for-one with the shirts thrown in for free. His jet-black shoes, also expensive, were so buffed and shiny that you could use them as a shaving mirror. All I knew for sure about the sparkling diamond-and-gold watch he wore was that it kept time to the billionth of a second. Who wants to be late when you're called to meet your Maker?

"Welcome," John began. "Would your driver like to step inside?"

"Oh, no, he's quite content. Listens to the radio."

"Is he on salary or indulgences?" John wondered aloud. I wondered silently if the Rev would indulge our sarcasm.

"He's a good friend of the church," the reverend replied, taking the snarky remark in stride.

"That would make him a BFF," I commented. "Emphasis on the last 'F.'"

"BFFR." The Rev clapped back, slowly pronouncing each letter. He was young enough to know the meaning was 'be fucking for real.' Even so, the usage of a profane initialism took us by surprise. He then stated the obvious as we headed to the solarium. "You are a very big man, John."

"Will that be a problem fitting me through the pearly gates?"

"No worries. Saint Peter holds the key and only lets your soul in."

"No corporeal body?" I protested. "That clinches it. I'm definitely not renewing my Peloton membership."

The Rev chuckled, saying, "You should be more concerned about the shape of your soul. Do you not know that you are God's temple and that God's spirit dwells in you?"

"Scripture?" John asked.

"The second sentence is," he glibly replied. "First Corinthians."

"You have a verse for every occasion?"

"Many."

"My birthday is coming up," John said.

"'Teach us to number our days, that we may gain a heart of wisdom.' Psalms."

"Impressive."

Yes, very, I thought. The Rev was quick with the quotes. But two could play that game. "'What does God need with a starship?'" I countered, adding a reference: "Kirk. *Star Trek* Roman Numeral Five." Two dozen such lines were stored in my memory banks, mainly from the original series. Hell, we all have our strong points.

By now, the reverend had seated himself and accepted a cup of Earl Grey. What else do you serve a church dignitary in the mid-afternoon besides tea and crumpets?

John and I had prepped for the visit. We were not so jaded as to deny that a man of the cloth can be sincere. Even inspirational. But as the Bible says, no one can serve two masters: God and money. Based on our research and his appearance, the Rev was a 'man of the cloth.' The only thing is that he had chosen Armani and Vicuña. Moreover, he seemed unconcerned that his spendthrift ways were on display for all who chose to see. Rather than deny it, he had embraced the lifestyle, managing quite well by feeding off those who are vulnerable and easily duped. How such excesses are sustained is hard to comprehend until you consider the math: Even a small percentage of a large number of people can equate to success.

"I had not realized," the Reverend said, "that we are practically neighbors. I think God has smiled upon us both."

"Are you sure," John said, "that's not a grimace you see?" We had learned that the Rev lived in a nearby McMansion. "'In my Father's house, there are many rooms.' I guess you didn't wish to be outdone."

I expected, even wanted, a combative reaction, but didn't get one. How disappointing. The Rev was not only immune to remarks about his display of personal wealth; he had a ready retort. "Do you know anything about the Catholic Church's wealth?" he asked. "How much real estate, artifacts, paintings, gold, and corporate investments that it owns? Few know the exact amount; it's too big and diverse to estimate. But let's be charitable—forgive the word—and say tens of billions of dollars. All untouchable and untaxable. As for myself, I have enough to be comfortable."

"Your self-discipline is commendable," John said. "Throw in a few miracles, and you'll qualify for sainthood."

"There's also martyrdom," I suggested.

We were finally getting under the Rev's scales. "Did you have a specific purpose in mind," he asked, "when you invited me here today?"

"We'd like to reach an understanding," John said, "concerning your sermonizing in support of Congressman Hargrave. You must recognize that he is a man of questionable moral character."

"We are all sinners in God's eyes. Perhaps, if we were to judge fairly, some more so than others."

"And yet you encourage your congregation to vote for him. Why?"

"Because he is a humble man. He came to me seeking forgiveness for his shortcomings—such as they are."

A look of understanding slowly swept over John's face,

replaced by disgust.

"So Caesar is rendering unto you?" John said.

The Rev was too clever to say what he wanted directly. Instead, he asked: "Do you have any transgressions you'd like to confess?"

I was eager to answer first: "Does the thought of drowning you in a font of holy water count?"

The Rev attempted to leave. John stopped him. "Pardon my irate friend here, but I can assure you he means no harm. I am more contrite than he—and as you can see by looking around, well-off."

With one wary eye on me, the Rev returned to his seat.

John continued: "I propose to make a sizable contribution to your ministry."

"In return for?"

"Merely for you to do nothing. No more sermonizing on the current election. Favor no one. That is all I ask. Agreed?"

The Rev looked carefully at John and nodded. The simple nod would not suffice. I understood why. As I said, we had prepped for the meeting.

"Should I get my checkbook?" John prompted again. "Are we in agreement? There will be no more politicizing from the pulpit?"

"Agreed," the Rev said.

John turned to me. "All good?" he asked.

"Hundo P," I said.

From the start of John's odyssey, I had kept a compact recorder in my pocket, though I never would have guessed that it would be used quite this way. I placed it on the table directly in front of the Rev, who, unspeaking, eyed the little black box warily. He was about to see religion but was still in denial, so I picked up the device and replayed the last nifty bit for him to hear.

"You intend to bribe me with that?" he asked with an uneasy laugh. "You've heard of the separation of church and state? The government doesn't care what I do from the pulpit. The IRS is too afraid to hassle me."

"Perhaps. But that tape and a public statement from me will do you far more harm than the IRS ever would," John said. "Your donations will dry up faster than shite passes through a goose."

"I seriously doubt that," the Rev replied. His expression said otherwise; he was having difficulty believing himself. Pity: Belief in himself was the only faith he knew.

"Are you prepared to find out?" John asked.

"What do you want?"

"For you to do what I asked ... and you agreed to do," John replied. "Absent my contribution to your 'ministry,' of course."

"What's your angle in this?" the Rev asked. "You don't like Hargrave, I get that. What's in this for a man like you?"

"Let's just say I want to keep my better angels happy."

We walked out to the Rev's limo, the type where a soundproof partition physically isolates passengers from driver, rich from poor. I marshaled the driver's attention with a knuckle rap on the front-side window. Opening the window, the man greeted me with a look of tolerance mixed with disapproval. I gestured to the back seat, where the Rev was preoccupied with his cell.

"What do you see in that asshole?" I asked.

The driver, surprised, scrutinized me. Without missing a beat, he answered.

"I see a man, no matter where I faithfully take him, who has lost his way."

As the limo sped away, I turned to John, who had been listening.

"Damn him," I said, referring to the driver. "Just when I thought I was justified in disliking everyone again."

What John said next stuck with me:

"That's the problem with generalities."

17. MOOSE

THE REVEREND COMPLIED WITH John's 'advice.' What, if anything, had been accomplished (other than our entertaining ourselves) was difficult to determine. The Congressional race, however, was now characterized as a 'statistical dead heat.'

October arrived, ushering in cooler weather. Of all the seasons, the advent of fall had always instilled in me a heightened awareness of the passage of time, much more so than any arbitrary holiday or birthday. Nature's cycle of assurance, exuberance, temperance, and abstinence is that of life itself. My personality finds temperance the most sobering. In this, I am not entirely alone. There is a battle to be waged as we cope with the unfathomable mystery of existence.

We all have our ways of maintaining sanity.

Sensing the general mood, John suggested—and we all eagerly agreed—that we abandon the 'burbs for a cabin in the country. After a three-hundred-mile journey, we arrived at the Adirondack Mountains, where the sky claims its own shade of blue, and the air is still crisp and sweet as a New York apple. Not far away was Ithaca. If an odyssey needed an ending, nearby was as good a place as any.

I regret how, in the twenty-first century, it's hard to find yourself in what qualifies as the middle of nowhere, though, parenthetically, the middle of nowhere is exactly the best place to find yourself. For us suburbanites, our idyllic mountain location came damn close. It speaks volumes when you can make kids forget the internet.

Looking back, there have been transformative changes in the last few months. John, physically, of course. Looking inward, I saw a subtle change in myself: a tolerance, no, a *need*, for the company of others.

Happily, there were also changes in our bank accounts. Money can't buy happiness, but taking a loan on it is a distinct possibility. The cabin we rented had everything we desired: a bedroom for John and Amanda, another for Jessica and me, and one each for the children. There was a timbered ceiling with a massive iron chandelier and a stone fireplace big enough to roast a cow. Above the fireplace's hewn oak mantel was mounted an odd-shaped bow. Best of all, thanks to twelve heavily wooded acres and a thousand feet of lakefront, there was the isolation we craved.

We arrived mid-afternoon, weary and hungry from the trip. The lateness of the day was reason enough to forgo the day's hiking to chill on the deck and fire up the six-burner grill. We brought two big coolers of food, including juices for the kids and fermented juices for the grownups. Long Island vineyards produce some exceptional white wines.

After dinner, the conversation turned to the next day's hiking.

"Do you think we'll see a moose?" Brad asked, hoping.

Looking at John, I knew, based on our hiking experiences, that a simple answer would not suffice.

"Well, son," he said, "I really hate to disappoint you, but moose are long extinct."

"No way," Brad responded. He and his sister were old enough

to separate fact from fiction.

On the other hand, who among us does not have, after finishing a good novel or leaving a great movie, a slightly altered view of reality, if only for a short time?

"Sorry, Brad," I said, "but your dad is right. Species Furicatus Amerinaus is, sad to say, no longer with us."

Amanda, trying to stifle a laugh, choked on her wine. "I see," she managed to say. "We have a resident moose expert here."

I ignored her. "Gone like the dinosaurs," I continued. "Of the hundreds of trails your dad and I have hiked, in Vermont, in Maine, even in marsh areas commonly, but erroneously, referred to as 'moose country,' we have yet to observe a single, solitary moose." (That was true.) "I'm afraid they don't exist."

"Well, *I've* seen one on TV," Carrie protested. "My friend's dad has seen one."

"Same," Brad said, supporting his sister. "So, how do you explain *that*?"

"You've both been to Disney World," John answered. "Where you've seen the realistic-looking animals that look, move, and act like the real thing. They're all animatronic. People see that when they think they see a live moose."

Jessica chimed in. "You might ask your dad why on earth anyone would take the time and energy to place an animatronic moose in the middle of nowhere. In the middle of a lake!"

John frowned as he stalled for time. Finally, he asked: "Do I really need to explain that to anyone?"

"Sorry, partner," Amanda chimed in. "I think we all do."

"Tourism," John said, sounding like the idea was as apparent as the lake sparkling in the diminishing light.

"Hundo P," I insisted, but I had no clue why. "Tourism."

"Yup, tourism," John repeated. "Who wouldn't love to see a real live moose!? Everyone wants to get a glimpse of one. The mere chance attracts tourists, which, of course, is good for business."

"And that, folks," I said, "explains who and why someone would pay to put an animatronic moose in the middle of a lake."

John and I were treated to a chorus of raspberry noises. Seeing that we had convinced no one, John had this to say: "Hey, I'm quite willing to be proven wrong. Tomorrow, we'll go on a long hike where I've been told moose have been sighted."

From the vantage point of the cabin's deck, we watched in the fading light as the kids explored the lake's shoreline. The ghostly call of a loon echoed across the water. Reacting to the solitude inherent in such settings, Jessica snuggled against me. Being close to her, comforted by the company of my dearest friends watching their children play, was doing a stellar job of dispelling my usual feeling of isolation.

I purposefully caught Amanda's eye, then looked at Jessica and mysteriously said, "Do you think we should tell them?"

"Seems only right," Jessica responded. "We can surprise the kids later."

I focused on Amanda. Despite John's size, she was the bigger target. "We want to share something with you." That was sufficient to get her attention.

"No way?!" she shouted.

"Way," I said.

"Way," Jessica echoed, pointing to the modest band on her ring finger.

"Yeet!"

Amanda's shout got John's attention. "What's going on?" he asked.

"They're engaged!"

Jess and I rose to accept congratulations and for Amanda to admire the ring.

John stared at me, the startled expression on his face replaced by a broad smile. He took one long stride to where we stood and encapsulated the three of us in one group hug.

"I love you guys," he said.

He wasn't the type to abuse the word; I'll admit a tear came to my eye when he said it. It's funny how one tiny drop of water can signify feelings too big for words to explain. But I managed: "You might say Jess and I meeting was almost as accidental as yours with Amanda."

"Some people claim," Amanda offered, "that everything happens for a reason."

"So they hope," John remarked.

"I want to believe, my dear, that there is a reason for what's going on with you. After all, Jess and Max would never have met."

"Don't forget about that boatload of cash," I said to a chorus of groans. In fairness to us, we did give a portion to good causes.

Jessica had more to contribute to a high-key day. "There's more news, John," she said, alerting us with her 'Doctor Whitmore' voice. "News you might appreciate. Your height has decreased by five millimeters—eleven total now, establishing what appears to be a trend."

"If there's one thing I'll never grow out of, Jess, it's appreciating your kindness and support." Then, smiling while gesturing at me: "And somehow your tolerating Max here."

John always did have a way with words.

The kids were excited by the news of the engagement. After Carrie stopped shrieking, we regrouped in front of the fireplace, playing board games to a background of firewood snapping and sparking. One game, *As Funny As*, challenged players to invent jokes from random cards. John started with 'Name tags at a Where's Waldo Convention.' Carrie made us laugh with 'As Funny as a Zebra Named Spot,' and Brad earned high points for 'As Funny as a Porcupine at a Petting Zoo.'

With no regrets we could detect, Jess and I would never have kids. Maybe I felt the planet didn't need the extra burden. Maybe, if I took a closer look, I couldn't manage the selflessness. John and Amanda, however, had made us part of their family—a level of responsibility I could willingly embrace.

We ventured onto the deck, reclining on chaise lounges to gaze at the night sky. Pollution and light pollution had yet to reach here, leaving the mountain air clear enough to see the broad expanse of the Milky Way. To Brad and Carrie, I pointed out the smudges of galaxies.

"Who of us doesn't feel small contemplating that," John said, transfixed.

"This is my religion," I added, looking up.

Maybe the kids didn't know what I meant.

In time, they would.

The next day, we were two miles into the hike when, partially hidden by foliage and the morning mist, was what appeared to be a moose.

18. CHINA

Upon returning to society, John (who deliberately had not accessed his phone or laptop for the several days we were vacationing) opened an email that originated from the Chinese Embassy in New York. The body of this communication is below:

Most sincere greetings! We hope you are in good health and high spirits.

You may find some comfort in knowing that we recently identified three citizens of the People's Republic of China who may have acquired the same difficulty as you. They have adjusted well, and we are much gratified that one has exceeded your maximum reported height and weight. Our great scientists can assure that these citizens began their remarkable transformation long after you. We are diligently researching possible causes and see no evidence of person-to-person transmission.

You are most welcome to visit, and we are inviting you to bring whomever you choose to meet these people and compare experiences. We stand ready to help in any way necessary. Please feel free to contact the Consulate General at our New York embassy. He has been authorized to provide all the travel arrangements for you and your party and help resolve any concerns.

There is no obligation to bring your complete medical record, although we

see mutually beneficial cooperation in your doing so.
   We look forward to seeing you soon.
   Best wishes

After verifying the letter's authenticity, John asked me, "Would you like to visit China?"

"Are they known for having a sense of humor?"

"They have their own flavor of sarcasm. I'm pretty confident we're up for the challenge."

"I'm in. And the ladies? The kids?"

"Anyone wishing to go."

"Sounds perfect," I said. "If meeting these three people does nothing else, you might get a measure of solace from seeing that you are not alone."

What John said next, I'm still learning. But it's getting better.

"Well, Max, the way I see it, none of us are."

Before departing for China, an autocratic state, we learned that Jackson had won a close election. When and whether he'll be seated in Congress is another matter. The result is being contested. Call this the new normal in a cray-cray world. As I said before, the struggle is real.

Regarding John's disorder, as of this writing, the cause has yet to be discovered.

I can tell you that the Squad had a celebratory party when he broke below seven feet.

Many others, however, voiced disappointment that he didn't just keep growing.

Praise for Gary Tarulli's novel, Orb

There's intelligent life in this SF yarn—a smashing beach read. --Kirkus Reviews

"Orb is highly satisfying for a first novel. The scientific questions raised are not cliché and the author deals with them in a mature but entertaining manner. Recommended for anyone with a thirst for good character study or deeply speculative science fiction." -SFRevu

"A story of close quarters and the psyche, "Orb" is an intriguing pick for those who like science fiction with a psychological edge." -Midwest Book Review

"I think what kept me hooked the most was the element of suspense woven seamlessly throughout the story. There was always the question of 'What next?' in the back of my mind." -Red, Red Reader Reviews